"I've been thinking, too."

Curious, Amy peered his way. "Thinking? All by yourself?" Why not give Beau a taste of his own medicine?

He surprised her with one of his charming grins, and a tiny tingle raced through her at the sight. "Don't be bashful," he coaxed, lounging casually against the tree. "Tell me how you *really* feel."

"Maybe we'd better go inside."

He moved into her path. "Wouldn't you like to know what I've been thinking?"

His face was silhouetted against the soft moonlight. "Uh—actually, Mr. Diablo, I don't think I need to know."

"I was thinking, since I won't be attending the wedding, maybe I'd better kiss the bride—now."

Dear Reader,

I'll get in the mood here and say, "Howdy!"

How the West was wooed! I love that slogan. But it's going to take some doing for Beau Diablo to woo Amy Vale. First, he hates her before he ever lays eyes on her. Second, she's engaged to someone else. So wooing, in their case, looks pretty hopeless.

That's exactly the scenario for romances I love the most—an impossible situation with an utterly devastating hero and a perfectly lovely, though misunderstood, heroine. They think they can't stand each other, but are forced to spend days and nights in close proximity. Yep, that's my favorite. And I had a good time bouncing this couple off each other—in the snow, at a barn dance, in a sleigh, under a wintertime moon. Even once while she was in the bathtub, but I don't want to tell too much!

Add to that mix cowboy boots, tight jeans and a gorgeous man mounted on a big, black stallion. Picture him glaring down at our spirited heroine, completely out of her element, but who simply can't be cowed—and, well, I'm in romance heaven.

Being from Oklahoma, where cowboys are thicker than the smoke from a wet wood fire, I had lots of fun writing *To Lasso a Lady*. Beau and Amy became special to me, and I hope their romance will be special to you, too. So, whether you know anything about the American West or not, and even if you don't care a speck about cattle ranching, sit back, put your feet up and come along with me to wintertime Wyoming to meet Beau and Amy. I think you'll enjoy their perilous and amusing venture into love—as well as the whole HITCHED! series!

Happy trails, partner!

Renee Roszel

To Lasso a Lady
Renee Roszel

Harlequin Books

TORONTO • NEW YORK • LONDON
AMSTERDAM • PARIS • SYDNEY • HAMBURG
STOCKHOLM • ATHENS • TOKYO • MILAN
MADRID • WARSAW • BUDAPEST • AUCKLAND

With love to my son, Doug

ISBN 0-373-03397-4

TO LASSO A LADY

First North American Publication 1996.

This edition published by arrangement with Harlequin Books S.A.

® and ™ are trademarks of the publisher. Trademarks indicated with
® are registered in the United States Patent and Trademark Office, the
Canadian Trade Marks Office and in other countries.

Printed in U.S.A.

CHAPTER ONE

THE tall stranger exploded through the entrance of the country store, accompanied by a wail of cold wind and battering snow. Even after he shoved the door shut behind him, a foreboding chill seemed to linger in the air.

His stance was rigid, waiting, somehow angry. His arms were poised away from his body, as though it were high noon in the Old West and he expected to have to shoot it out at any second.

Amy had enough problems and needed to decide what to do quickly, but she couldn't resist an urge to scan the man's face and see if it went with the tough-as-nails image of his Western gear. Even though the small grocery store was flooded with stark, fluorescent light, she was disappointed to find his features shaded by a black Stetson. Still, the bright lights provided a spectacular show. The melting snow along the shoulders of his split-hide rancher's jacket and wide-brimmed hat glittered and winked like washed diamonds.

Now this man, she mused without hesitation, *is a real guts-and-leather cattleman*. He wasn't one of the citified pretenders who frequented the Chicago cowboy bar where she'd been a cocktail waitress for the past four years. This man, in his scuffed boots and well-worn jeans, was the real thing, and her heart fluttered with feminine appreciation.

He yanked off his hat and slapped it impatiently against a leg. Amy followed the motion, noting jeans so close fitting she could see saddle muscles bulge and flex in his outer thighs. She had no idea where she'd heard that term—saddle muscles. Probably somebody at the bar had mentioned how you could tell a real cowboy from a fake. A real cowboy's thighs were overdeveloped from long hours in the saddle. She swallowed hard at the stimulating sight, unable to recall seeing a pair of male legs quite that nicely contoured—except maybe in Olympic events—especially considering this cowboy's thighs were swathed in a layer of denim.

When he plowed a gloved hand through his mane of black hair, her glance followed, and she was startled to discover his eyes were aimed her way.

His glare was bold, defiant, the flinty blue of the wintry sky outside. Before she could react to the hostility in his stare, he'd snapped his wide shoulders around and was intent on searching the throng restlessly milling in the store.

Most of the stranded bus passengers were lined up at the establishment's only pay phone, scrambling to make arrangements for emergency lodging or calling relatives to say they'd be delayed. Roads north and west had been closed by the Highway Patrol because of a snowstorm.

Amy heard the crunch of boots on the gritty wood floor and realized the cowboy was stalking off, apparently having located his prey. She watched him round a rack of paperback books, heading toward the line of travelers gathered before the phone. He moved with solid grace, a man in total control of himself and his world. But she could tell he was reining in his emotions with difficulty, for his square jaw was working, his nostrils flaring. She pitied the person who'd put him in his rabid state.

Dragging her attention from him to her watch, she nervously began to chew her lower lip. Ira was a half hour late, and he'd left no message that he'd been delayed. She wondered if Diablo Butte was affected by the snowstorm and if she should try to get a room at the local motel—if there was a local motel. Though this western Wyoming community was called Big Elk, the only thing that seemed very big about it was its name. From the bus window, she'd seen no buildings for miles except for this clapboard general store and the gas station across the street.

She supposed it didn't really matter if Big Elk had a motel. She was low on funds, with exactly seven dollars and thirty-three cents in her purse. That wasn't enough for a cheap room in a ghost town, let alone in a tiny dot-on-the-map community jammed with panicky people whose options were shrinking as a nearby snowstorm held them hostage.

The bus driver had given the passengers the choice of going back with him to Kemmerer to get a room there, then resume their journeys when the storm passed and the next bus came through. Or, if their destinations allowed it, they could take a more southerly bus route out of Kemmerer. He'd said he'd wait another thirty minutes for anybody who wanted to go back with him.

Amy didn't know if the bus company would charge for taking them back to Kemmerer, considering this was an emergency. Probably. The storm wasn't the bus line's fault. If they did, she couldn't afford it. Besides, this was *her* stop. Ira was to have picked her up here to take her on west to Diablo Butte, her new home where she planned to build a new life as a rancher's bride.

She peered at the fidgety people waiting for the phone, wishing she'd tried to call Ira earlier. From the number still lined up to make calls, it would be another half hour before she'd even get the chance.

She noticed the tall stranger again as he edged up beside a stack of soft-drink cases. Perched cross-legged atop the stack was one of the passengers who'd been on the bus with her. Amy didn't know the woman's name, but had found out quite a bit about her, even so. She'd occupied a seat directly behind Amy and had spent almost every waking minute since she'd gotten on the bus, bumming cigarettes and talking to anybody who'd listen about her budding career as an exotic dancer, and how she was on her way to fame and fortune in Hollywood.

Amy wondered what this lanky, tough-as-rawhide cowboy had in common with a woman whose nostril was pierced, whose bleached hair was cut so short she could be in the Marines—except for one blue ponytail protruding above her right temple. She was wearing a stretch, zebra-striped bodysuit, white patent leather boots and a fake-fur leopard coat. They were as unlikely a pair as Madonna and John Wayne. Amy wondered if the cowboy had a kinky streak and if he picked up women this way very often.

The Madonna look-alike blew smoke out her nose and shook her head, causing her blue ponytail to wag back and forth across one heavily made-up eye. The cowboy nodded and turned away, his hooded gaze sweeping the store again. *Well*, Amy reflected, *either the woman isn't into gorgeous cowboys, or he'd asked her some other kind of question.* She had a feeling, if he'd actually been trying to pick her up, she'd be walking out of the store clinging to his coat sleeve right now. Evidently she hadn't been his quarry after all.

Amy told herself the cowboy wasn't her business. She had to figure out what to do. Ira was probably on his way, but she really should call his ranch and make sure everything was okay. She only hoped it wasn't long distance, for that would eat up too much of her dwindling funds.

She didn't feel as though she ought to call him collect. That was a silly idea, she supposed, since Ira *was* her fiancé. Naturally, he'd accept her call without hesitation. And he was certainly wealthy enough.

She balled her hands, hesitating. She absolutely didn't want Ira to believe she was marrying him for his money. He'd admitted he'd had bad luck that way in the past. No. She wanted to prove to him she was sincere in her desire to be a rancher's wife, and that when she took the vows, they would be forever. And she wasn't his wife yet. Wouldn't be until Valentine's Day, three days from now.

Since that was the case, somehow even a collect call seemed grasping. She wanted to prove herself first. Show her earnest desire to make their marriage a solid, honorable partnership before she started accepting material things from him, even small things—like collect calls.

She glanced hopefully out the store's window, hoping she'd see her cheerful fiancé—a man in his late fifties, yet charmingly young at heart—ambling toward the door. Her hopes faded. All she saw beyond the dingy glass was snow and more snow, swirling and dancing in the late-afternoon gloom. *Well*, she mused unhappily, knowing she had little choice now, *there was always the chance that Diablo Butte was a local call—*

"You must be Miss Vale," came a deep observation at her back.

Startled to hear her name, especially spoken in such a churlish tone, she spun around. For one instant, she had the bizarre notion she was expected to apologize for who she was. *How crazy!* Clearly she needed sleep.

The first thing she registered was a black bandanna, tied below a deeply cleft chin. In a square-cut jaw, a muscle flexed furiously. The broad shoulders of a split-leather coat were familiar, and realization hit like a club. Her gaze shot upward, clashing with eyes that were deep blue and as angry as when he'd first entered—maybe more so. Amy couldn't understand what this furious cowboy might want with her.

"Why—why, yes, I'm Amy Vale," she said, her voice peculiarly weak.

The eyes flashed with some caustic emotion, but it was quickly squelched. With a half smile that was far from friendly, he said, "I've been sent to fetch you for Ira. He's snowbound."

Amy experienced a rush of disappointment, but wasn't really surprised. Her whole trip west had seemed to portend nothing but disaster, with rain and snow dogging the entire route. Though she'd tried to push the thought aside, that very fear had nagged at her since she'd arrived here and her fiancé was nowhere to be found. "Well..." She exhaled tiredly. "I—I appreciate your offer, but I couldn't accept, Mr.—Mr...."

He settled his Stetson on his head, adjusting the brim low on his brow as he looked around. "Where are your bags?" he asked, apparently not registering her refusal.

"Excuse me, but I said I couldn't accept—"

"I heard you." His belligerent gaze snagged hers again. "Lady, I don't like this any more than you do. But Ira asked me to pick you up, so I'm picking you up. It'll take us nearly an hour to get to my ranch headquarters, even if the snow doesn't get worse. So where are your bags?"

She heard a muffled "thunk" and became aware that she'd stumbled backward into a shelf of canned goods, knocking one off in her defensive retreat. She flattened herself against the display, gaping at him, utterly confused. He was towering there too closely, invading her space. His obvious animosity and threatening nearness alarmed her. Everything about him radiated dislike, even disgust. There was *nothing* mixed in that signal. This cowboy didn't like her. Not one bit.

Amy had been born and bred in the big city, and like any large municipality it could sometimes be heartless and unfeeling to a young woman trying to make it on her own. She'd deflected the unwelcome advances of her share of jerks over the years. But faced with the cold fury in this cowboy's eyes, it took her more than one attempt to find her voice. "I—I'm going to give you five seconds to back off, mister," she warned unevenly. "Or I'll—I'll scream."

A dark brow arched, and for a moment he examined her with mistrust. He peered around, and Amy guessed he was deciding that even as big as he was, he'd have trouble fighting off ten or twelve rescuers who were already in a bad mood.

Clearing his throat, he took a step away from her and crossed his arms over his chest. "Look, Miss Vale," he stated less curtly, apparently concluding that his "I'm the bull and this is my grassland" attitude wasn't going to work with her, "I'm not the neighborhood kidnapper. I have a ranch west of here, and Ira asked me to put you up for a few days until the roads open." He pursed his lips, clearly an attempt to bridle his temper. "I'm pleased to do it for him," he finished thinly.

She didn't relax. His cordial act wasn't fooling her, but she had no idea how to react. Screaming didn't seem quite right any longer.

"Now, ma'am," he drawled, placing a finger to the brim of his hat in a gesture that was more mocking than gentlemanly, "if you'll show me your bags, we have a long drive ahead of us. If that storm turns our way, we may have more than our share of problems getting home."

She continued to eye him with suspicion. In her job, she'd seen lots of overbearing, manipulative types, but this guy was in a class by himself. Just because he *said* he wasn't the neighborhood kidnapper didn't mean a thing. "Just a second." Having made her decision, she spun away. A few steps had her at the cash register where a paunchy, balding man in a green flannel shirt was grinning ear to ear, overdosing in delight at the flurry of junk-food and cigarette sales he was making to the stranded wayfarers. "Excuse me, sir?" She waved to get his attention over the dull roar of voices.

When he aimed his protuberant eyes her way, she gestured toward the cowboy. "Do you know this person?"

The proprietor's glance swung to the tall, range-rugged man and back to Amy. "Beau?" he asked, looking puzzled. "Sure."

"Then he does own a ranch around here?"

The man's grin widened, displaying big white teeth that would have been more at home in a horse's mouth. "I'd say so, miss. If ya call eight hundred thousand acres a ranch."

She blinked at the size. She assumed the proprietor was being sarcastic, but, even if he wasn't, eight hundred thousand acres sounded big to her. Nevertheless, the vastness of a ranch wasn't exactly a character reference. "Is he trustworthy?" she asked, beginning to feel silly. It was clear this uncivil rancher was known in the community. And it was laughably apparent to anyone who cared to take a casual glance at him that he was gorgeous enough to have women falling all over themselves to give him whatever he might want. If he ever chose to be the slightest bit charming, he wouldn't need to resort to force. Still, his manner was so—so—menacing. It was better to be safe than sorry.

The storekeeper looked once more at the cowboy, who had ambled up beside her. She could detect his after-shave—wood smoke and pine. Nice.

With a guttural laugh, the proprietor rang up a couple of candy bars for another customer, then kidded, "I guess to answer your question, miss, I ain't never heard no complainin' about ol' Beau." He winked in the cowboy's direction. "Especially not no *women*."

Beau grunted, appearing more annoyed than amused by the good-old-boy compliment. "Miss Vale," he ground out, drawing her unenthusiastic gaze. She stiffened, hoping the heat in her cheeks didn't denote a blush, but afraid it did. She was embarrassed beyond words at what the proprietor had implied about this stranger and his prowess with the ladies. Her glance skittered across his handsome face, but she avoided his eyes, apprehensive that she'd see something more bothersome in their depths than anger—very probably amusement at her expense. "What?" she finally asked, studying her nails and noticing her hands were trembling. She jammed them into her parka pockets.

"We don't have time for games." His tone was grim. "As I said, I'm doing Ira a favor."

"Pretty reluctantly, I'd say."

"Very reluctantly, Miss Vale."

Disconcerted by his bluntness, she jerked to stare at him. He was observing her through shuttered eyes. "By the way, the name's Diablo. Beau Diablo."

She couldn't have been more shocked if he'd tossed a handful of sand in her face. "*You're* related to Ira?"

"Yeah." He worriedly scanned the plate-glass window as a burst of wind-driven snow battered the panes.

She was dumbfounded by the news. This man was nothing like the fun-loving, jovial gentleman she'd met in Chicago. Yet, even as different as the two were, surely Ira wouldn't entrust her with anyone dangerous. "Mr. Diablo, why didn't you tell me—"

"*Dammit!*" He shifted to pin her with a threatening stare. "Miss Vale, you have five seconds to show me your bags, or we're leaving without them."

*   *   *

As Amy huddled in the warm cab of Beau Diablo's pickup truck, she felt as though she'd been sentenced to an eternity in The-Purgatory-of-the-Perpetually-Angry-and-Silent. She had no idea how much time had passed since they'd left Big Elk, but she prayed the trip would soon be over. She was getting a cramp from pressing herself against her door.

She'd relegated herself to a small section of the truck cab for two deeply disturbing reasons. First, she preferred to put as much distance as she could between herself and her ill-tempered host. Secondly, Beau's wide shoulders rudely took up more than their share of space, and she had no intention of being thrown against him every time they hit a bad spot in the road.

Trying to calm her frazzled nerves, she stared out the side window at the passing scenery of rolling hills. They were glazed with several inches of snow, punctured occasionally by statuesque stands of firs and pines. The blowing flakes seemed more lovely, cleaner, out here in this primitive Wyoming splendor than they did from the window of her tiny apartment over the pawnshop in Chicago—or from Mary's sterile-smelling hospital room.

Poor, dear Mary. She forced back a growing depression. Her little sister was recovering from surgery—hopefully her last—and the convalescent home was very nice. As soon as Mary was well enough, and the bills were paid, she would join Amy and her new husband on Diablo Butte.

Mary was so courageous. Amy already missed her spunky smile. A melancholy sigh escaped her throat and she cast a sidelong glance at Beau, wondering if he'd heard. His intent expression didn't indicate that he had, so she shifted to look away.

She supposed she could scream, clutch her chest and collapse into a lump on the floorboards and he wouldn't react. In all the time since they'd left Big Elk, he'd said nothing, hardly moved. He'd just sat behind the wheel, staring into the gathering darkness, eyeing the gravel road between labored swipes of the windshield wipers. Every so often he flexed his gloved hands as though he were gripping the wheel too tightly and his fingers were cramping.

She heard the sounds again of leather clenching and unclenching, and peered at his profile. He'd deposited his hat into the storage area behind the seat along with her suitcase, for he was too tall to wear it inside the truck's cab. His hair was slightly mussed. A wisp brushed his forehead, softening the frown that seemed to permanently reside there.

He had a strong face, she mused, with cheekbones straight out of the "Bone Structures For The Rich and Famous" catalogue. She scanned his eyes and wondered why she'd always thought of long, curling lashes to be the sole domain of high-fashion models. Beau Diablo proved that notion false, for his thick sweep of lashes in no way diminished the masculine allure of his face. And the five-o'clock shadow of dark whiskers along his tense jaw completed a sinfully handsome picture.

Life wasn't fair, she brooded. Why did such an arrogant, bossy man have to be so appealing? He didn't deserve to be, but he no doubt used his good looks to their full potential when it suited him—which clearly *wasn't* now.

Irritated by the turn of her thoughts, she shifted in her leather seat, restlessly smoothing her beige twill slacks. For the first time, she realized how wrinkled and dingy they looked after the two-day bus ride. Even worse, her tan parka was spotted with dark stains where one of her bus seatmates had sloshed coffee on her somewhere in the middle of Iowa.

Casting her companion a hesitant look, she fought an internal battle. The last thing she wanted to do was broach any subject at all, let alone ask him a favor. She knew she'd have to do it sooner or later, so with a deep breath she plunged. "Do—do you suppose I could wash some clothes while I'm staying at your place?"

Barely turning his head, he flicked her an aggravated look but didn't speak.

Exasperated, she rolled her eyes toward the roof of the truck. "Look, Mr. Diablo, I suppose it's your business what sort of manners you cultivate—or *don't* cultivate. And if being a disagreeable pain in the neck works for you, it's none of my business. But I think Ira would at least expect you to be *civil*."

He surprised her with a chuckle, though it was the most bitter excuse for laughter she'd ever heard. "Miss Vale, Ira expects me to keep you from freezing to death. That's all."

She bounced around to glower at him. "If you hate the idea of a houseguest so much, why didn't you say *no*?"

He pursed his lips, then to her surprise, actually glanced her way, his gaze raking her face. "Because he threatened me."

"Oh, right," she scoffed, picturing her kindly, middle-aged fiancé threatening this powerful young stud. "What did Ira threaten to do? *Shoot* you?"

"No." He turned back to maneuver around a curve in the slick road. "Visit me."

Amy was taken off guard by his wry answer. She knew it was a ludicrous reaction, but she almost smiled. "Very funny." She snapped away to watch the wipers dispose of accumulating snow. "Okay, I may not be the brightest person in the world, but I can tell that you and Ira aren't close. What are you, some sort of distant, black-sheep cousin or something?"

He flexed his fingers, a sure indicator the question bothered him. "Not exactly."

When he didn't reveal more, she glared his way, determined to get a straight answer out of him, or die trying. "Please, don't make it easy for me. I've got nothing better to do. I'll just *guess*. Let's see, you're a cattle-rustling nephew?" Pretending to be deep in thought, she shook her head. "No—no, it's coming to me. Could you be his dipsomaniac uncle? No. That's not quite right. Let me think...." She tapped her cheek as though this was an earth-shattering dilemma she was bound to solve. "I have it. You're his transsexual *sister*-in-law!" She eyed him narrowly. She could keep up this foolishness if he could, darn him. "Nope. Nope. Nope," she babbled on, "now that I see your earlobes up close, I'll bet you're his demented half brother out on bail for the ax murder of—"

"I'm his son, Miss Vale."

He'd spoken so quietly she wasn't sure she'd heard right. For a long minute, all she could do was stare at his forbidding profile. Finally, she managed, "You're his *what*?"

The truck slowed as he braked. When they came to a stop, he faced her. Resting one arm on the back of his seat, he leaned across the console, looming very close, too close. Though his bracing scent beckoned, his eyes were as hard and cutting as steel. "We're home—*Mom*." Scorn twisted his lips. "What's for dinner?"

CHAPTER TWO

THERE was nothing physically threatening about Beau's closeness, but somewhere deep inside herself, Amy grew fearful. Something she couldn't even guess at seemed suddenly very wrong.

Though his revelation about being Ira's son shook her, she managed to scramble from the truck before he could open her door for her. She had no intention of causing him one more second of inconvenience than she already had. But she was too late to get her suitcase; he'd grabbed it up when he retrieved his Stetson.

As he came around the truck, he planted his hat on his head. His rough-cut features were solemn yet extremely engaging—too engaging for a future stepson. She forced her glance away and focused on the house. Snow was drifting down around them and dusk had fallen, but the brass lantern lighting the porch gave her a muted view of his rustic and rambling home. Made of logs and set picturesquely amid a copse of snow-mantled hemlocks, it was more enchanting than she'd imagined a remote ranch house could be.

The roof was gabled with deep overhangs. A wide porch was supported by heavy columns of whole tree trunks, bark and all, making the house seem to blend magically with the towering evergreens that embraced it. Amid the falling snow and haloed porch light, the

20

place had an unexpectedly warm appeal, paradoxical considering the coldness of the man who owned it.

There was a grip at her elbow, and Amy came out of her trance, allowing herself to be towed along a meandering stone path, then up three steps to the long porch. "I'll leave you with Cookie," he muttered over the hollow thud of his boots on the wood planking. Swinging open the rough-hewn door, he deposited her suitcase in the entry. "Go on in," he said, as a tall, thin woman in jeans, boots and bright wool shirt hurried along a side hall toward them.

"I'll take her from here, boss." The woman smiled and waved, as though she knew he was in a hurry. "She'll be fine. Don't you worry."

Before Amy knew what was happening, the woman had scooped up her hand. "Come along, honey." She grinned. "I figure you'll want to clean up and change before you eat. So I won't waste no time with prattle, now. We'll talk later, over stew and biscuits."

Amy didn't know what she'd expected, but it certainly hadn't been anyone quite so friendly and breezy. "Why—thank you. I do feel pretty grubby."

The woman laughed, a croaking, happy sound. "You look as fine as them mail-order catalogue gals, but I know how traveling can tucker a body out. We'll take care of that in no time." She squeezed Amy's hand. "I'm Cookie. I pretty much take care of Mr. Beau's house. You'll meet Archie, my mister. Best cook in the state—to hear him tell it." She croaked out another splintery chuckle. "He does fry up the best mountain oysters in the state, if I do say so. But don't never let him hear I said it. He's hard enough to live with as it is, the ol' coot."

Amy had no idea what mountain oysters might be, but the woman was chattering nonstop, giving her no opening to ask. Besides, Western dishes were the least of her worries right now. She stared at the animated woman beside her, gray hair pulled up in an untidy knot. Her face was long, nut brown and seamed from wind and sun. The creases around her small violet eyes and thin lips hinted at a perpetually sunny disposition, and she wondered at how difficult that must be, working for Mr. Picklepuss.

They'd walked through the entry hall and descended two steps into the living room where a massive stone fireplace dominated. She swept her gaze around in awe, noting rough beams and rafters, earth tones and furnishings hewn straight from the forest.

As Cookie chitchatted about what a shame it was the bad weather had stranded Ira on Diablo Butte, they exited the living room and went along a hall where a striking Navajo blanket dominated the log wall. After a right turn, Cookie announced, "Here's your room, hon." She deposited the suitcase by the door, and the sound it made scraping the cottonwood planks was the first time Amy realized the woman had picked it up. Embarrassed, she said, "Oh, I'm sorry. I didn't think about my bag."

Cookie appeared puzzled. "Your bag?"

She indicated her suitcase. "I—I didn't mean to make work for you."

Cookie's laughter rang out again. "Hon..." She shook that head full of flyaway gray. "Takin' care of houseguests is my job." She stepped back from the room's entrance and nodded toward an interior door. "That there's the bathroom. It opens on the hallway, too, so take care to lock that outside door if you don't want no surprise company.'' She put a hand on the doorknob. ''Now you get in there and take a relaxing bath. Supper'll be ready for you when you're ready for it.''

The door clicked shut and Cookie was gone. Amy scanned her surroundings—homespun and serviceable. The bed's headboard was ingeniously simple, fashioned out of three curved branches. On the far side of the bed was a modest writing desk, and the chair that sat beside it was formed with more branches, the seat and back covered with cowhide.

The window curtains were of coarse linen, matching the bedspread, and throw rugs were woven from colorful rags. A knotty, peeled stump served as a bedside table, and the reading lamp was fashioned from an old-time wagon-wheel hub.

This place was a far cry from the steel-and-Plexiglas world of Chicago. Yet, even as sparsely decorated as Beau's home was, it had a dignity and strength, a sense of self, that was all its own. She was impressed—*completely against her will*—since it so obviously reflected the distinctive taste and independent spirit of her antisocial host. And since he was so unimpressed by her, she had no desire to be impressed by anything about him.

Amy looked up from her book, thinking she'd heard someone enter the living room. Apprehension tingled along her spine when she realized it was her host. His hair, damp from a shower, glimmered in the fire's flicker and she noticed that same unruly wisp that had been out of place in the pickup was trailing across his forehead, giving the false image that he was nonchalant and friendly.

She wondered if he did that on purpose to attract unsuspecting women into a night of wild debauchery before they really got to *know* him, or if his hair was as obstinate as he was, and he couldn't quite control it. She smiled inwardly, hoping that was it. She'd like to think this ill-tempered cattleman didn't have control over *something* in his world, and that, maybe, he lived every day of his life tromping around in coiffure hell.

His footfalls resounded as he crossed the polished floor, but grew muffled on the massive Southwestern rug that anchored the seating area before the hearth. Amy swallowed nervously, wondering if he was going to take a seat beside her on the couch.

He passed by without a glance, picking up a fireplace poker and nudging the burning logs into heightened frenzy. When he ran his fingers through his damp mane, sweeping the wayward lock into place, Amy's buoyant mood vanished. So much for her wicked fantasy life.

She opened her mouth to speak, but couldn't seem to find her voice. She swallowed several times, wondering at herself. Why was she so nervous? He turned away to pull a log from an arched alcove in the stone wall, and she surreptitiously scanned him, wondering why his every move drew her interest. He had a rotten disposition and a hateful attitude, and he didn't deserve one second of her attention.

His damp hair gleamed in the firelight, and she grew irritated at how attractive he looked in the flame's glow. He'd cleaned up and changed into fresh clothes. The bulky white turtleneck he was wearing only served to accent the thickness and breadth of his shoulders. His jeans were freshly creased, yet every bit as snug against his thighs as those he'd worn earlier. His boots were different, too. Polished and light tan, they looked as soft as glove leather. She bet they were custom-made and more comfortable than the furry slippers she was wearing.

She hadn't heard him come into the house, and was startled to find him joining her at this late hour. She knew it was after ten, for the mantel clock had chimed a few moments ago. Of course, it was *his* living room. He had every right to enjoy his own fire any time he pleased. She should have stayed in her room if she'd wanted to dodge his company. Unfortunately for her, the scent of wood smoke had beckoned so strongly she'd weakened and come in to curl up on the thick, slubby cushions of the pine couch.

After a delicious dinner of elk stew, she'd spent a peaceful couple of hours before the fire, reading the book she'd brought with her. She had to admit, Beau Diablo's home was an absolute dream, with all the warm, honey-golden wood—until *he* walked into a room with that ever-present anger in his eyes and turned it into a smoldering nightmare.

He hadn't seemed surprised to find her here, but didn't smile in greeting when their eyes met. She was getting used to that glower by now so she tried not to let it get under her skin. For the past couple of hours, she'd tried to convince herself that her host wasn't such a bad guy. Both Cookie and Archie seemed quite fond of the man. So she reaffirmed her vow to give him the benefit of the doubt. Maybe he didn't dislike her at all. Quite possibly he had a really bad hangnail that was making him cranky, or he'd just been informed he was being audited by the IRS. Everybody had bad days. She'd probably met him at an unfortunate time, that was all. She would try to hold on to that thought no matter how hard he glowered at her.

After replacing the poker beside the other fireplace tools, he took a seat in one of the matching, rust-colored armchairs that sprawled on the opposite side of a unique coffee table. Amy had admired it when she'd come into the room. Constructed of twisted, fossilized wood supporting a square slab of thick glass, it was more like artwork than mere furniture. She'd thought the table had been enormous, but when Beau stretched out his lanky legs, crossing his ankles beneath the glass, the massive barrier seemed puny.

"Evening," he said minimally as he settled in, his darkly sensuous gaze roving over her.

"Good evening." She smiled, trying to mean it. For some reason, his piercing stare made her feel underdressed, though that was ridiculous. She was perfectly respectable in her navy, velour warm-up. She was proud of the outfit, as a matter of fact. Nobody would ever be able to tell she'd bought it for practically nothing at a secondhand store, for she'd mended the rip in the leg so carefully it wasn't detectable. She had nothing to be ashamed of. Still, as he perused her from the tips of her fuzzy slippers to her straight hair, freshly washed and pulled back in a loose ponytail, she felt as though she should run to her room and put on a coat.

When she realized he wasn't going to say anything more, she pondered what she should do. He turned away to glare into the fire, making it clear he wasn't in the mood for idle chatter, so she tried to go back to her reading. After five minutes of scanning the same sentence, she was frustrated to discover she had no idea what it said. *Where was her mind?*

The fire crackled and popped, a restful sound that should have eased her nervousness. It wasn't working. She didn't have any idea she'd slid her glance back to Beau's face until she became conscious of the fact that he was watching her. With a surge of discomfort, she decided she had to try to chip away at his bad mood. She'd always had a knack of coaxing people into a smile. Maybe Mr. Diablo just needed to get his mind off whatever was bothering him. She cleared her throat. "You have a lovely home."

Fixing an elbow on one knotty chair arm, he rested his chin on a fist. His frown didn't waver and he didn't respond.

She fidgeted, unprepared for such rudeness. In her job, she'd dealt with bad manners and knew there were a few people in the world who were terminally uncivilized, and there was little that could be done about them. Still, she decided not to give up quite yet. After all, she was his houseguest. "Oh, thank you, Amy," she quipped, as though he were responding to her comment. "I built it all by myself. I'm such a *manly* man." She spread her arms as if to show off the room. "I didn't chop down these trees, you know. I chewed them with my strong, manly teeth!"

He cocked his head, squinting slightly. She couldn't tell if he thought she'd gone insane and he should call a mental hospital, or if he'd found what she'd said barely entertaining. Whatever he might have thought, he made no comment.

With a rankled sigh, she decided Mr. Diablo might be one of those terminally rude people. Readjusting her book, she tried to read again. The words blurred, seemed somehow foreign and unintelligible. She

started a paragraph several times, but it was no good.
Her mind was simply not on reading.

The fire hissed and snapped and the wood smoke
invaded her senses like a kindly old friend. Inhaling
deeply to compose herself, she caught another scent.
It was subtle, a clean smell. She breathed it in, trying
to guess what it was. After a second deep sniff, she
decided it must be Beau's fresh-from-the-shower
scent. Wincing, she rubbed her eyes. She didn't need
this.

He was so quiet for so long, she couldn't stand it.
As far as she could tell, she had three choices. She
could either try again to engage him in conversation,
leap up and scream "Are you trying to drive me
crazy?"—or simply leave. The idea of leaving seemed
best, but she didn't think rudeness on her part would
solve anything. With a heartening inhale, she opted
to try one last time to draw him into civil communi-
cation. After all, even beasts of the jungles and for-
ests had been domesticated over the centuries. Why
not this glowering brute?

She met those stormy eyes with reluctance. "I—
I've been reading about Wyoming," she began, trying
for a topic she hoped might spark his interest. "And
I was surprised to read that the first women's suffrage
legislation was passed here in 1869, and that Wyoming
had the first woman governor in the United States."
She paused to take a breath, praying he'd respond.

His gaze went on impaling her. "Uh . . ." She cast
about mentally to find anything to fill the awkward
breach. "The Equality State, right? I mean—that's
what Wyoming's called. Sounds like this is a great
place for women." She tried to maintain a pleasant
facade, but her mind was shrieking, *Apparently,*

boorish stinkers are in the minority in Wyoming! Just my luck I'd be stuck with one!

His eyes narrowed suspiciously, as though he was reading her thoughts, but he didn't speak. Aggravated, she eyed heaven. "I'm impressed, Amy," she chirped, answering for him again. "Did you read all that on the bus? You've got quite a strong constitution. I usually get carsick and barf when I try to read on a bus." She uncurled from the couch, sitting forward as though in animated conversation. "How enchanting, Mr. Diablo. I had no idea you were a bus-barfer. And people say you're not a sparkling conversationalist."

He sat back, running a hand across his mouth, then simply watched her again with eyes that were shuttered and unreadable.

Feeling about as foolish as she ever intended to feel, she slid her gaze away toward the fire. *That was it! Nobody could say she hadn't tried!* "You know," she muttered more to herself than to him, "in some radical segments of our society, people actually *answer* other people. It's considered polite."

"But you were doing so well all by yourself."

She jumped at the sound of his voice. After the silent treatment, she'd resigned herself to expect nothing but a closemouthed glare from him for her entire captivity.

She had a feeling her expression must be almost cringing, which was certainly an overreaction. After all, he'd made a simple statement—however mocking. He was Ira's son, not a deranged maniac with knives for fingernails. "W-what?" she asked, sorry the question had come out in a high-pitched squeak.

He placed his elbows on the chair arms, templing his fingers before him. "Bus-barfer, Miss Vale?" His eyes were hooded, and his tone gave away nothing. She couldn't tell if he was amused or irritated.

She shrugged. "Sorry. I'm new at talking for everybody in a room. Maybe if I stay here long enough, I'll get better."

"It's good to have goals," he taunted quietly. Lowering his hands, he sat slightly forward. "I understand my father called you this evening."

She was startled by the abrupt change of subject, and for some reason his choice of topics made her restless. On the plus side, at least he was speaking to her. She nodded. "Y-yes. He said he was up to his ears in snow, but he was his usual cheerful self."

"I'm sure," Beau muttered. "And I assume you told him I was the perfect host?"

She could detect his sarcasm, but didn't rise to the bait. "Of course that's what I told him." It wasn't her habit to speak badly of people who did her a favor, however grudgingly.

He lifted a skeptical brow. "And did he seem surprised?"

Actually, Ira had called her a sweet little liar, but she didn't want to make matters worse by admitting that, so she shook her head. "Not a bit," she lied.

His lips quirked. "Don't ever play poker, Miss Vale. You'd lose your shirt."

She dropped her gaze to the rug of bright maize and chocolate brown, with splashes of rust. It was a striking floor covering, but she was too uncomfortable to appreciate the decor right now. He was right. She didn't lie well. She could hardly deny what must be apparent in her troubled features.

Unhappy with the current subject, she leaped to a new, safer one that had been on her mind. She glanced at him. Well, not quite at him, more past his shoulder toward the wall of windows some distance away. There was nothing but a black void beyond the glass. "I— was wondering," she began tentatively. "Doesn't Beau mean 'handsome' in French, and Diablo mean 'devil' in Spanish? And if that's true, doesn't that make your name Handsome Devil?"

"Does it?" An eyebrow rose inquiringly. "I wonder why no one's ever pointed that out to me before."

His mocking tone made it clear his quixotic name had caused him no end of trouble over the years. And watching him in the flickering firelight, she had to admit that no matter how much inconvenience his name had caused him, it couldn't be closer to the truth. *He was a handsome devil.*

Now that she'd studied him closely, she could see that he was every bit his father's son, similarly handsome, only more so. Taller, darker, with the long-limbed, muscular build of a man who lived a life that required much from him physically.

She was surprised at herself for feeling any affinity for him at all, considering how unfriendly he'd been. Unsettled by her contrary emotions, she looked away, gritting her teeth.

"Where did my father meet you, Miss Vale?"

The question was completely unanticipated. She assumed Ira had at least told Beau that much. Apparently they never talked to each other, and she wondered what had caused such a rift between father and son.

She heard a flutter-flap, flutter-flap, flutter-flap, and noticed she was anxiously fanning the pages of her

book. The mention of her job occasionally caused
eyebrows to rise. It didn't happen much, but it happened enough to make her self-conscious.

She sat up straighter and closed the book, placing
it beside her. She had nothing to be ashamed of and
made unflinching eye contact. "I was a cocktail
waitress in a Chicago cowboy bar. Ira went there every
night for the two weeks he was at that cattlemen's
conference last December."

Beau made no comment, but he pursed his lips, a
cool inference that she was guilty of something. She
bristled. *That was the look she hated*! She'd met
people like Beau Diablo before—intolerant, judg-
mental types who believed that just because a woman
worked in a bar she was cheap and easy.

The truth was, the tips were good, and with her
parents' insurance money gone and her sister's medical
bills mounting, she needed all the cash she could
scrape together. So, she made a living serving drinks
to pseudocowboys who liked to shuffle around the
dance floor doing the "Cotton-Eyed Joe" and the
"Boot-Scootin' Boogie." That was hardly evil.

Indignation bubbled inside her, but she tried to keep
her affront from showing. Her mind tumbled back to
when she'd first seen Beau Diablo in the little grocery
store that afternoon. He'd been furious, and he'd gone
straight to the exotic dancer. She began to think the
two things might be connected, and asked, "Since you
didn't know anything about me when you came to
pick me up, I'm curious about why you asked the
woman with the blue hair if she was me?"

He half grinned, but there was no humor in the
expression. "Because she looked the most like Ira's
last three wives."

His revelation stung. "Ira told me he'd had some bad luck in the past with wives, but that's over!"

His gaze narrowed, and Amy had a feeling he didn't buy that for a minute. "Whatever," he muttered. "When Ira described you to me, he said you'd be wearing your hair in a ponytail, so—"

"So you naturally assumed it would be *blue*?"

He grunted out a chuckle, clearly surprised to find her able to make a witty remark. "Ira also mentioned you had brown eyes and blond hair. The woman with the nose ring matched that description." He casually crossed his arms before him. "Your hair isn't that blond, Miss Vale."

It was now painfully clear why he'd been so hostile. It hadn't been a stomachache or stopped-up sinuses or anything of the sort. He just plain didn't like her, or what he perceived her to be. The fact that Ira's son could be so narrow-minded came as a blow. She pointedly turned away. "Sorry if I don't *exactly* fit your stereotype of a bloodsucking bimbo."

There was a drawn-out pause. "Ira also told me you were beautiful," he added flatly.

She swallowed with difficulty, her throat dust dry. *So naturally you decided to talk to every other blonde in the store before you came to me!* she fumed silently.

She couldn't understand why this stranger's opinion bothered her, but it did. Tired from lack of sleep, she was quickly reaching the end of her rope. "Just for the record, Mr. Diablo, your thoughts on the subject of my *looks* don't interest me in the least. I detest men like you, who put people into neat little heaps—nice girls here, bad girls there, computer nerds behind the sleazy lawyers! You didn't have to meet me or get to know me. You'd already made your decision about the kind of person I am." She hated the fact that she'd let him get to her. She hardly ever lost her temper this way, but she couldn't seem to stop the angry words from pouring out. "As far as you're concerned, I'm a trampy bubblehead grabbing a meal ticket! Well, you're one hundred percent wrong, Mr. Diablo. *One hundred percent!*"

Though her motives for marrying Ira were far different from what Beau believed, the fact that she didn't love her fiancé would only make any explanation she might give seem as contemptible as if she really were becoming his wife for his money. In truth, she intended to make a lasting commitment to Ira, but she had no plans to explain herself to this insolent man.

She had no desire to go into her reasons for getting married, or of explaining that, after Ira had gone to the cowboy bar every night for the two weeks he was in Chicago, he'd stunned her with a proposal of marriage. Of course, she'd thought he'd been kidding, but he'd been so sincere, so refreshingly chivalrous, she'd finally believed him.

It had seemed like the answer to a prayer for both her and Mary. And as Amy and Ira exchanged one chaste kiss, he'd promised he would never ask anything of her that would make her uncomfortable with her decision to marry him. He'd said he'd learned from his past mistakes and was looking for companionship, pure and simple.

Amy was looking for someone nice to spend her life with, someone honest who could make her smile. She'd never been in love, and wasn't even sure such an emotion existed. Passion, as far as she was concerned, was highly overrated. It was a solid, trusting partnership that counted and that's what she wanted. Ira had even offered to pay for Mary's convalescence, promising she could join them when she was well enough. Amy could almost say she loved Ira for that act of kindness alone.

So, let Beau think whatever he wanted—he would anyway. Why waste her breath telling him her marriage to his father was to be a platonic match? It was her business and Ira's business how they planned to live their lives, not Beau's! "I've already told your father, and now I'm telling you." She jumped up. "I plan to be the *best* rancher's wife in Wyoming. Any other plans Ira and I have are none of your business!" She grabbed up her book, then threw him an odious glare, deciding it was time he got a taste of his own medicine.

He didn't seem chastised by her outburst, and that made her even angrier. Was there no way to get to this man?

"The best rancher's wife in Wyoming?" A sardonic grin tugged at the corners of his mouth. "Who are you trying to convince, Miss Vale? Me—or you?"

The query was as hurtful as a slap, and she gasped. "Your father is completely different from you. He's so—so accepting."

Beau pushed himself up to stand before her. Even from the far side of the coffee table he seemed dangerously tall, ominously close. "If you mean he accepts every woman he meets in a bar as his bride, then I have to agree with you."

She was so horrified she couldn't respond. How crude! How rude he was! In all her twenty-four years she'd never met a man as unredeemably loathsome as Beau Diablo.

"I apologize if I seem severe," he said, his tone far from repentant. "My father is a grown man, and you're obviously a grown woman. And you're quite right, your plans are none of my business. You're welcome here as long as necessary." With a slow, unsmiling nod, he pivoted away, murmuring, "Evening."

She stared speechless as he ambled away. When he reached the hall, he turned back, thrusting his hands into his pockets. His stance looked elegantly casual, but she wasn't fooled. His disdain for her was as hot and palpable as the fire that raged in the hearth. She lifted a belligerent chin, positive he would be astute enough to detect her dislike for him, too.

He chuckled, and the sound was harsh in her ears. Yes, he'd received her message loud and clear, and it hadn't even fazed him. "Miss Vale," he drawled, "John Ruskin once said the most beautiful things in the world are the most useless." He paused, and she watched as a muscle flexed in his lean cheek. "Just for the record, I think you're very beautiful."

A heartbeat later he was gone. Amy stood there feeling like she'd been dashed with a bucket of ice water. His eyes had glittered with such utter contempt, she couldn't move. The man had told her she was beautiful, yet she'd never felt so insulted in her life. Even standing before the blazing fire, she found herself shivering uncontrollably.

Amy was awakened by a tapping on her door. She rubbed her eyes and yawned. It was so dark she couldn't see a thing. "Yes?" she called sleepily.

"Hon?" Amy thought she heard a tinge of pity in the female voice, and couldn't imagine why. "Mr.

Beau said to wake you. Seems he thinks you have a hankerin' to help with the haying and chopping ice.''

Amy rose up on an elbow, confused. She had no idea what either of those things were. "He—did?"

The door clicked open a crack, and in the yellow light from the hallway, she could see the flyaway-gray head of the housekeeper. "There's hot coffee, buckwheat cakes, steak and eggs for breakfast."

Amy couldn't imagine anyone eating that much food, especially in the middle of the night. Yawning again, she wriggled up to sit. "What time is it?" she asked, brushing hair from her face.

"Five, or there'bouts."

Making a pained face, Amy squinted at the luminous dial on her travel clock to make sure she'd heard right. Five-o-three, to be exact. Shaking her head, she tried to clear the cobwebs from her brain. The last time she'd looked at that clock it had been four-thirty. She hadn't slept well, her inability to settle down probably due to the fact that she was used to getting off work at two o'clock in the morning. It was close to four many mornings before she crawled into bed. At least that's what she hoped the reason was. She didn't like to think Beau Diablo had invaded her dreams, making her restless and upset even in sleep.

She stifled another yawn. She would rather spend another evening in front of a fire being glared at by her host than get up now. But she had a sneaking suspicion why he was doing this. She'd told him she wanted to be the best rancher's wife in Wyoming, so he was giving her a taste of what ranch life was like. The underhanded sneak! "Okay—sure." She rubbed her eyes. "How long do I have?"

"Mr. Beau wants to be in the truck and movin' by five-fifteen."

She was sliding her feet over the side of the bed and into her slippers, but she stopped dead. *He was giving her ten minutes to dress and eat*! Keeping any negative thoughts to herself, she nodded. "I'll hurry."

"Hon," Cookie said, "have you got some nice, warm longhandles?"

Amy exhaled wearily. "What kind of handles?"

The door opened wider. "Didn't figure you knew about those. Here. I got plenty. You take these. And I brung you some heavy socks and other warm gear. You need to layer up in this cold."

The housekeeper seemed concerned, not her smiling self, and Amy took pity on her. "Don't worry about me, Cookie." Putting on a brave face, she threw off her covers. "If Mr. Diablo wants to give me a feel for ranch life, then I'm thrilled about it. Honestly." She shuffled to the door and took the bundle of clothes. "I'll be ready for breakfast in five minutes."

Cookie nodded and smiled, but a trace of pity lingered in her expression. "I don't rightly know what's going through Mr. Beau's head, Miss Amy. That ain't no work for a little city gal like you."

She smiled wanly. "Cookie, I have a feeling that's exactly his point."

CHAPTER THREE

FOUR minutes later, Amy was at the kitchen door, her head held high. She was not going to give Mr. Beau Diablo a single thing to fault her about. When she pushed through into the brightly lit room, she was surprised to find Cookie sipping coffee all alone before a stone fireplace. Disconcerted, she asked, "Am I late? Have they already left?"

The housekeeper smiled. "Shucks, no, hon." She put her mug on the long table and hurried toward the kitchen's back door to retrieve a battered old field coat from a hook. "They're in the cook house. Mr. Beau usually eats breakfast with the hands, bein' a bachelor and all." She took down Amy's freshly washed parka and beckoned for her to follow. "I'll show you the way."

Once Amy was bundled against the cold, she and Cookie stepped out into the dawning day. The cold was so bitter, it staggered her. Her step faltered. "How cold is it?" she asked, watching her breath freeze in the air.

"Oh, 'bout fifteen below."

"Below? *Freezing*?"

Cookie let out one of her splintery laughs. "Zero, hon. Not a bad day. No wind." They trudged along a gentle slope away from the ranch house in about three inches of snow. "If the sun comes out, it'll get up near zero."

Amy swallowed. "That's nice." It got cold in Chicago, too. But she didn't spend her days out in it. Her stinging ears reminded her to pull up her parka hood. Fifteen below zero! She clutched her hands together apprehensively.

The view was hazy with falling snow, making the cloudy dawn seem to be brushstroked by an artist's hand. And the silence. How could a place so vast be so quiet? Amy took a deep breath. Though her lungs froze, she delighted in the smell. Sweet, pure, cold. It was a refreshing change from the city's exhaust and pollution, even if it was a little on the deathly cold side.

Though much of the landscape still lay in relative darkness, the fallen snow provided luminescence, and she could see a scattering of buildings silhouetting the landscape. Farther away, behind wooden pens and a log barn, the rolling hills were forested with stands of pines.

Cookie touched her elbow. "This is me and Archie's place." She waved toward a quaint log cabin not far from the main house. "On the other side's the cook house and then the bunkhouse."

Amy noticed that all of them were of the same pine-log construction, their roofs blanketed by an icing of snow. Smoke curled from each chimney, and she could smell it. The whole experience was wonderful. Like a scratch-and-sniff Currier and Ives painting.

"You go on in the cook house, hon. I've gotta stop by my place for some cleanin' supplies. It's that plank door, there."

Amy nodded her thanks and tromped along the path of footprints already marring the pristine snow. With every step her stomach knotted tighter. She looked down at her running shoes and shook her head. If her feet didn't freeze off today, it would be a miracle. They were already numb.

She heard a general hum and rumble of male voices when she got to the door, but the instant she stepped inside, the room went still, ten pairs of male eyes turning in her direction.

Amy stumbled to a halt, embarrassed to be the center of attention. She felt like a bug that had just appeared in the middle of somebody's birthday cake. Surprise seemed to be the expression of the day, except for Archie-the-cook's squinty old gray eyes smiling at her. She didn't see Beau, and it was clear that her unwanted presence on his ranch hadn't been passed on to the hired help. She wondered where he was.

The cook house was long and rustic. Devoid of frills like curtains or seat cushions, it seemed perfectly fitted out for brawny cowboys. The ten-foot table, made of pine planks, was flanked by two long benches, and sat before a soot-blackened rock fireplace. The fire flickered warmly amid delicious mingled scents of homemade bread, hotcakes, strong coffee, scrambled eggs and steaks. Beyond the table where the cowhands gathered were the kitchen appliances—two industrial-size ovens, cooktops and refrigerators—tucked neatly in and around the rough log walls.

Amy heard someone clear his throat; it sounded like crushed rock banging down a metal chute. Her gaze swung to the table. The scene there was almost comical. Denim-and-flannel-clad cowboys sat or stood in a frozen tableau, halted in the act of swabbing up the last dab of maple syrup with a crust of bread, or gulping down a final swig of coffee.

The throat-clearing sound came again, more loudly this time. Amy saw movement, then, as Archie went on pouring coffee into one leathery-faced cowpoke's mug, she heard him say, "Mornin', Miss Amy." He grinned in his bashful way. "Come on over here and get yourself some hot coffee."

She smiled at the weathered cook, but before she could take a step, there was a thunderous scraping sound as the benches were pushed back and the hands abruptly stood. A couple of men who'd donned their ten-gallon hats in anticipation of leaving, grabbed them off and crushed them respectfully to their chests.

"Men. This is Miss Amy Vale," came a deep voice that she recognized as her host's. She heard another scrape of wood on wood and saw Beau as he rose from a hard-backed chair in a dim corner. "Miss Vale will be staying with us until the roads west are clear."

Amy smiled as the men timidly grinned and mumbled guttural greetings.

"Now that the pleasantries are over," he cut in, "Marv, you, Homer and Willie get those extra round bales to the north pasture. J.C. and Snapper, you do a ride-through to check for cattle that need doctoring. Buddy and Chick, make sure the creek water's open. Ed. You come with Miss Vale and me in the old pickup."

Amy watched Beau as he barked out orders, slipping a black down vest on over his black wool shirt. It jolted her when Archie shoved a thermos into one hand and a small brown sack into the other. "I fixed you a scrambled egg sandwich. And the coffee'll warm your innards." He grinned, and his sun-dried face crinkled like withered leaves.

"Thanks," she whispered. Tucking the thermos under her arm, she gave his callused paw a squeeze, then noticed the ranch hands were clomping out the far door. "I'd better go. I think I'm expected in the pickup."

"It seems so." Archie crossed his arms over a stout belly, giving his boss a dubious squint as Beau planted his Stetson on his brow. When he turned to face them, his eyes were shadowed, but there was no masking the spark of antagonism that hovered there. "Are you ready, Miss Vale?" he asked, his tone less a question than a dare.

Though she'd been scared and unsure of herself when she'd walked in, his challenge turned her into a rock of determination. Did he think a little Wild West browbeating would frighten her off? Not likely! She'd been living on her own and caring for her invalid sister for the past five years. If he thought she couldn't handle cold weather and a few disagreeable chores, he was nuts.

She marched across the room to where he was standing beside the wooden coat hooks. "I thought you'd *never* ask, Mr. Diablo." Her smile was as sweet as she could coerce it to be. With barely a glance in his direction, she breezed out the door.

As soon as she was outside, a blast of knife-sharp wind hit her, spattering her face with needles of snow. She was so shocked by it, she stumbled to a halt, which was a mistake, for she found herself slammed into a very immovable object at her back. The unexpectedness of the impact made her tumble forward in the slick snow. Almost as quickly as it had begun, her forward motion ended as something strong encircled her middle.

"What in the—"

Hearing that growl near her ear, it only took her a split second to realize she'd run into Beau Diablo, and when she'd toppled forward, he'd caught her against him to keep her from falling. His arms held her tightly. His breath was coffee warm against her cheek, his legs and hips fitting familiarly against her.

"Miss Vale, don't people who live in Chicago know how to walk in snow?"

She yanked away from both his intimate hold and the unsettling feel of his body against hers. Turning to face him, she objected, "Surely you didn't expect someone as useless and beautiful as I am to be able to *walk*, too!" She didn't enjoy sarcasm, but, considering he'd only given her time to throw her hair into a quick ponytail and brush her teeth, no one in his right mind could call her beautiful this morning. It had to be obvious that she'd slipped on an icy spot. Anybody could slip. Even *he* had to obey the laws of gravity.

He frowned at her, his glance sliding to her jogging shoes. "What the hell are those?"

She followed his gaze. "In Chicago we call them shoes. What's the matter with them?"

He muttered something unintelligible and pivoted away to reenter the cook house. In a few seconds he returned, carrying something. Stooping, he grasped one of her ankles. "Lift your foot."

"I'll fall."

"Hold on to my shoulders, and lift your damn foot."

She could see now that he'd brought out a pair of fleece-lined rubber boots. Deciding he'd only snap her head off if she objected, she juggled her thermos and sack and placed a hand on his shoulder to balance herself while she lifted her foot. He quickly shoved on the boot. It was too big and swallowed her leg all the way up to her knee, but it was toasty warm. "Now the other one."

She mutely obeyed, feeling like a four-year-old child needing help getting dressed. When the other boot slid into place, she complained, "I've dressed myself for years, Mr. Diablo."

He straightened. "We can discuss your hobbies some other time. Right now, we have cold, hungry cattle to feed." Taking her by the arm, he aimed her toward a waiting pickup. It wasn't the one he'd driven to Big Elk. This one was older, battered, and a cowhand was stacking square bales of hay in the back.

A few minutes later, Amy found herself wedged between the two men, bouncing along a snowy path. Except for barbed-wire fences that ran along on both sides of them, she would never have guessed this was a road. They hadn't gone far when the fence grew to ten feet high, with slats of wood running vertically from the ground up. "What's that for?" She didn't realize she'd verbalized her question until she heard her voice break the silence.

Her query was followed by even more silence, until finally the cowhand named Ed turned their way and glanced skittishly at his boss, apparently assuming he'd answer. Amy looked at the cowboy, knowing full well her host didn't speak to her unless he had something he wanted to shout. She smiled at the cowboy and was startled to see a flush darken his already-boot-brown face. He fingered his droopy mustache, which was dripping melted snow. "Them's snow fences, ma'am. Helps keep the roads clear of snow in spots where there's a lot of blowin' wind.''

Amy nodded. ''My goodness. You must get some pretty high drifts here.''

He fingered his mustache again, and Amy realized he was nervous. She was puzzled. She could think of no earthly reason she should make him nervous. ''Sometimes six foot and more, ma'am.''

She shook her head in disbelief. ''Look, Ed, since we'll be working together, I wish you'd call me Amy.''

His squinty black eyes widened, and he gave another peek at his boss. But when there was no overt objection, he looked back at Amy and grinned. ''Sure— Miss Amy. I'd be pleased.''

She laughed. ''Amy, Ed. Just Amy.''

She heard the squeak of leather and shifted to see Beau's hands flex on the wheel. ''Ed. Get the gate,'' he muttered.

Almost before the words were spoken, the hired hand jumped from the truck and was sloughing through the snow to swing a metal gate out of their way.

Amy couldn't stand the suspense any longer and shifted to face Beau. ''What, exactly, are we going to do?''

He stepped on the gas and they bounced through the gate. When Ed opened his door, Beau said, ''You drive. Miss Vale and I'll pitch the hay.''

Ed's eyes widened again, and he stood there speechless for a second before he found his voice. ''Uh—boss? I can pitch it jes' fine.'' He was frowning, clearly aghast that the young woman was expected to do such a demanding, bone-chilling chore.

"You drive, Ed. The lady wants to learn about ranch life." Beau climbed out of the cab, making it clear he didn't intend to argue the matter. "Come with me, Miss Vale."

Amy smiled at the cowboy. "I really do want to learn." She only hoped she meant it.

He swallowed, and she could see his prominent Adam's apple bob up and down. "If you get too chilly, you let the boss know, now," he cautioned, his grimace never easing.

Fairly sure "the boss" wouldn't care if she turned into a female Popsicle before his eyes, she merely nodded and slid out Beau's side of the cab. When she got around to the back of the pickup, he was squatting in the truck bed snipping the wire from around a bale of hay. The snow had already dusted his shoulders and the brim of his hat and had left a light coating on the bales.

Amy heard a bawling sound and turned toward it. For the first time, she could see dark splotches over the rise. Hundreds of milling, meandering blotches vaguely shaped like cows. "Wow," she breathed. "There are so many—"

"Miss Vale?"

She spun back to see that he was now standing on the tailgate. Apparently the loose hay had muffled his approach. "Yes?" She took an involuntary step back.

He reached down. "Let me give you a hand."

"No thanks." Presenting him with her back, she sidestepped him and boosted herself up on the tailgate, then pushed up to stand. "Okay." She slapped her hands together to knock straw from her knit gloves, purposely scanning the stacked bales to avoid facing those stern eyes. "What do I do?"

She could hear him move, but refused to turn.

"Take this pitchfork, and as Ed drives along the draw, you pitch the hay out on the snow."

She plucked the pitchfork from his hand, again evading eye contact. "No problem."

"I'll be breaking up the bales for you."

"Lucky me." She hefted the pitchfork gingerly, trying to get a feel for it. "Do I start now?"

"Just a minute." He leaned over the side. "Okay, Ed. Start moving."

The truck lurched, but Amy was ready. She hadn't ridden the "L" train in Chicago for all those years without learning how to brace herself for staggering starts and stops. She had an urge to give Beau a smug smile but decided against it. The less eye contact they shared, the better she felt about it, and he no doubt felt the same way.

The truck went down an incline toward the roving clumps of cattle. Amy shivered just watching them. The poor things were huffing and puffing frozen air, looking pretty miserable.

"You can start any time," he said from behind her, and she realized she'd gotten lost in her thoughts. The first few pitches netted her only a strand or two of straw. She cringed, knowing Beau was back there scowling at her ineptness. Any second he'd say something like, "That's fine, Miss Vale. Those cows need to go on a diet anyway."

After a few attempts, she figured out how to keep most of the hay on the pitchfork, and then get it over the end of the truck and actually onto the snow.

Cattle were ambling up, ready to eat. She found herself pitching and pitching, faster and faster, worried sick that the cattle get enough food.

"Miss Vale, the stock at the far end of the draw are going to be irritated with you if they don't get any feed."

She inhaled, feeling oddly light-headed. Leaning on her pitchfork, she cast him a direct glance for the first time since she'd climbed into the back of the truck. "Don't be shy, Mr. Diablo. Be sure and tell me if I do anything *right*."

His expression was unreadable, and she turned quickly away, cursing herself for forgetting her own rule of ignoring him at all costs.

She tried to switch her thoughts to more pleasant things. The morning sky, though heavily overcast, gave off a pearlescent glow, and the snow was puffy and chaste on a sloping hillside dotted with spruce and winter-bare cottonwood. It was beautiful. Even under these less than perfect circumstances, Amy was falling in love with Wyoming, and it made her smile.

Digging out a forkful of straw, she thoughtlessly glanced in Beau's direction and her smile faded. It wasn't particularly bad lighting for him, either. Somehow his expression seemed almost agreeable, his eyes less antagonistic out here. Gritting her teeth against the foolish notion, she pitched the hay into the air, hoping both her technique and her speed were closer to his exacting standards.

"That's better," he said after a time.

She caught her breath, but tried not to display her shock in her body language. She took another forkful of hay and pitched it off the back of the truck, never uttering a word. Off in the distance, she saw a couple of cowboys on horseback picking their way through the milling cattle, and wondered if they were the ones Beau had told to check to see if any of the cows were sick. As far as she was concerned, they should be suffering from bad cases of pneumonia if they had any sense at all.

For a long time, she didn't hear anything but the lowing cattle, the twang of the wires Beau cut, and the crunchy sound of cold hay being broken up. Once or twice she was startled to see an entire bale fly over the side of the truck and break up when it hit the snow. Apparently her cow-feeding speed had dropped below Mr. Diablo's standards again, but she didn't intend to give him the satisfaction of knowing she'd even noticed he'd done anything. Though she was exhausted and a little dizzy, she picked up her pitching speed a little and tried to ignore the fact that he existed on the face of the earth.

"After we finish here, we need to chop ice off the pond."

With shrieking muscles, she pitched again, grateful he couldn't see her face. Chopping ice off a pond didn't sound like a warm thing to do, and she was freezing. Her arms were killing her, and she was getting more and more light-headed from hunger. But she would have to faint dead away and have her nose crack off and drop into his lap before she'd admit that.

"Are you tired?"

"No," she wheezed, watching her icy breath dissipate in the air as the truck moved forward.

"Are you cold?"

"Why should—I be cold?" She blanched. The sentence had been long enough for him to detect the gap where she'd had to take a gasping breath. And worse, her voice had *quivered*.

She heard a banging, and spun around before she remembered she wasn't going to look at him. She had to catch herself, and shook her head. Why was she so dizzy?

Beau pounded on the cab's back window, giving Ed the signal to stop. When he did, she stumbled again, but caught herself.

Before she had time to absorb what was going on, Beau had leaped over the side of the truck and moved around to the back. "Come on." He lifted his arms as if he expected her to leap gratefully into them.

She laid the pitchfork against the remainder of the bales. There were only seven or eight, and it surprised her that she'd distributed so much hay. There had been at least twenty when they'd begun.

When she turned back, she eyed his uplifted arms with hauteur, then shook her head. "I have a feeling you wouldn't help Ed down. Don't do me any favors." She dropped to one knee, but before she could slide off, he took her around the waist and lifted her down.

"Ed's accustomed to being at seven thousand feet. You look a little unsteady. Besides, it's time for a coffee break." His hands lingered on her for a second longer before he released her and took a step back. "Are you too dizzy to walk?"

She blinked at him, puzzled by the lack of hostility in his tone. Every fiber of her body was revved up for a fight, and she was in a belligerent mood. He'd worked her like an ox for the past hour, treated her like an indentured servant, and suddenly he was being—what? What was he being? *Nice*? "I—I can walk." She eyed him with high suspicion. "So, do you want me to hike back to the cook house for coffee cups?"

His lips twitched. "If you prefer. But I thought we could share the thermos lid."

A flush heated her frigid cheeks. The idea of sharing anything so intimate as a cup of coffee with this man troubled her.

"And you can eat your breakfast."

She was even more surprised that he remembered she hadn't eaten. He led her around to his door and opened it. "Slide in."

Ed had already shifted to the passenger side, so she did as he asked without argument. If she'd been forced to admit it, she didn't know how much longer she could have gone on without food. She was pretty shaky. She supposed the altitude was part of her problem, but she had a feeling she was more hungry than she was disoriented from thin air.

"Ed, get back there and finish haying."

The cowman was already half out of the cab. "Yessir, boss," he shouted, closing the door behind him.

Beau took off his Stetson and placed it behind the seat, then motioned toward the glove compartment. "Your breakfast's in there."

As Amy ate, Beau drove along the valley while Ed finished breaking up the hay and pitching it. She turned around to watch what he was doing. The cowboy was much better at the chore than she'd been. "This isn't Ed's first day of haying."

Beau grunted out a chuckle. "How can you tell?"

"He has a great wrist twist that looks like it might be hard to master." She shrugged, turning back. "Oh, well, I'll learn. Coffee?" With a start, she realized she'd spoken to Beau in a pleasant voice. Where had *that* come from? Most likely it was because she felt better having eaten.

"I'd love some," he said, without glancing her way.

She couldn't unscrew the thermos lid with her gloves on, so she slipped one off. She'd begun to thaw out, and once her skin was exposed to the warmth of the cab, she felt the sting of the blister she'd worn on her palm. She must have made a sound of dismay when she uncovered the raw flesh, for Beau glanced at her.

She flipped her hand over, not wanting him to think she couldn't handle what he was dishing out. Trying not to wince with pain, she went about her task.

"Damn useless city gloves," he groused under his breath.

"Yes, but don't you think they're *beautiful*?" she joked, then immediately wondered why she'd blurted that, of all things?

His thick-lashed eyes touched hers, and for the briefest instant, honest amusement seemed to glimmer between them. The intensity of the experience stunned her. Was there more in his glance than humor? Before she could be sure of all she'd seen, a frown rode his features again. With nostrils flaring, he shifted his attention back to his driving. "There's a first-aid kit behind your seat. You'd better see to that hand."

Swallowing thickly, she twisted away to stare out the window, but saw none of the snowy scene before her. An irritation spiced with uneasiness engulfed her. Something intense had flared behind those dusky eyes. Or had it? Her breathing was suddenly labored and her pulse quickened. Had she actually seen masculine attraction there? Surely not. *Definitely not*! It was crazy. The man didn't like her. And she certainly didn't like him.

More importantly, she reminded herself, she was engaged to his *father*.

Amy sighed, squeezing warm water over her breasts as she relaxed in a hot bath. Even the act of squeezing the washcloth hurt. She was sore all over from the hard, physical work she'd done today.

Opening her eyes, she inhaled the steamy, rose-scented water. Even with all the hard work, she was surprised to find she was basking in a glow of satisfaction. She'd kept up, and she'd discovered she enjoyed the exhilarating outdoor life—something, being a city kid, she'd never experienced.

Lifting her right hand, she looked at her red badge of courage. That's what she called her blister. It stung, but it wasn't too bad. Beau had bandaged it for her. He'd had a surprisingly gentle touch. Then he'd insisted she wear his fur-lined leather gloves the rest of the day. She didn't know how his fingers kept from dropping off in the cold, but she noticed a couple of the other cowhands were gloveless, too.

Sighing again, she shook her head. Maybe Wyoming cowboys' skin had mutated over the centuries to endure ice-age temperatures. That was the only answer she could come up with that seemed plausible to explain why those men hadn't left broken-off bits of fingers littering the pastures where they'd spent the day chopping ice from the pond, haying and doctoring the cattle for foot rot and some other revolting virus she couldn't recall.

Her eyelids began to droop, and she was amazed at how tired she was. Dipping her head beneath the water for one last rinse, she came up wringing out her wet hair. It wasn't even ten o'clock, but she had a feeling she'd fall asleep the instant her head hit the pillow. With both the physical work and the emotional battering her nearness to Beau Diablo had caused her, she didn't have an ounce of energy left.

Stepping out of the tub and grabbing a towel, she exhaled despondently. Her close proximity to Beau for so many hours had been a distracting experience—the smoky-pine scent of his after-shave, the warmth of his breath on her face every time he'd turned to talk to Ed, and worst of all, the feel of his torso crushed hard against her as the three of them bounced along on that fiendish bench seat that insisted on sloping in Beau's direction. By the end of the day, she'd been a worn-out, nervous wreck.

Beau, on the other hand, had been in total control, all business, never tiring. Unlike the other cowhands—who watched her, insisting on helping if she appeared confused or cold—Beau hardly seemed to notice she was alive, except when he shouted orders in her direction.

She toweled her hair more fiercely than she'd intended, muttering, "I'll show you who's useless, Mr. Beau Diablo!"

She heard a sound and looked up in time to see the hall door swing open. Hastily, she pressed her towel to her breasts to preserve her modesty as her eyes clashed with an all-too-familiar sultry gaze.

"What do you think you're doing?" she demanded, her voice a breathy whisper.

Beau had come to an abrupt halt. His eyes widening slightly, he mouthed an oath.

"I locked that door!" She fumbled to better cover herself.

"Sometimes the latch doesn't catch." He frowned. "I thought you'd gone to bed."

She gave him a look that made it plain she didn't believe him.

His expression altered from apologetic to annoyed. "I don't have to burst in on naked women to get sexual gratification, Miss Vale."

Amy didn't follow her urge to avoid the severity in his glare, and eyed him levelly. She was unstrung to her soul, standing there practically naked and totally vulnerable before him. But she was angry, too. How dare he loiter there debating with her.

She already knew he disliked her, but she hadn't missed the look in his eyes when he'd first stepped through the door. He might not care for her as a person, but he had *definitely* reacted to her as a woman, whether he'd meant to walk in on her or not. She wanted to get back at him for his hurtful remark the night before, and for his ungentlemanly behavior now. Her voice chilled and scathing, she challenged, "Who are *you* trying to convince, Mr. Diablo? Me— or you?"

His face and body grew rigid, and he frightened her by stalking farther into the bathroom rather than hurriedly leaving as she'd expected. Taking a protective step away, she found herself pinned against the tub. "What—what are you going to do?"

He paused, his flinty eyes raking her face. "Why, ravage you, of course."

Before she could protest, he'd scooped up several pairs of leather gloves that had been drying on a rack above the heater. He pivoted away, and a second later the bathroom door closed behind him.

Amy stared after him, her breathing shallow, a tight, mortified ache in her stomach. Why in the world had she intimated he was sexually attracted to her? Even though she'd been positive at the time she'd seen lust in his eyes, now she was afraid it might have been nothing more than a trick of light playing on his startled features.

Moaning aloud, she slumped to the tub's rim. Who did she think she was anyway? Sharon Stone's sexier sister? Dismay slid through her. *How could she ever face the man again?*

CHAPTER FOUR

AMY woke with a start from a nightmare where huge, howling wolves were using battering rams to break into her room. She rubbed her eyes and sat up, growing wary, afraid. Even though she was awake, she could still hear the wolves and their blood-curdling howls as they clawed and slammed into the walls and roof.

Terror clutched her by the throat, but before a scream could escape, she had grown alert enough to understand it wasn't an attack of rabid, giant wolves after all. It was the blizzard they'd been both expecting and dreading. It had finally turned south and was here, beating down on them with violent, frigid wings.

Instinctively, she jumped from the bed and threw on some jeans and a heavy wool shirt and raced to the kitchen. As she expected, no one was there. Biting her lip, she peered out the back door's window. A bawling wind shrieked beyond the frosted glass, blinding snow in its breath. As she stared in awe at the raw power nature could unleash, it slashed madly at the windowpane, a ferocious beast bent on getting at her and ripping her to shreds.

She stumbled a step backward in the face of such wild, yet dazzling savagery, but only for a second. She dared not dwell on it or she would lose her courage. Determinedly, she grabbed her parka and pushed open the door, forcing her fears aside. The wind pressed against the door, nearly throwing her to the floor, but she held on, finally managing to extract herself from the kitchen as the door slammed at her back.

Turning into the flesh-cutting snow, she pulled her parka hood close around her face and bent into the wind, heading for the cook house where she sensed she would find activity, and hopefully, something she could do to help.

The wind ripped at her and shoved her sideways and backward, twice knocking her to her knees, but at last she made it to the cook-house door. Once inside, she fell backward against the thick planks, using all her strength to get it closed.

After the raging storm, the relative silence of the cook house was almost deafening. She glanced round to see Cookie and Archie scurrying around the kitchen area while three of the cowhands sat at the table slugging down coffee and sandwiches.

"What in land's sake are you doing here, hon?" Cookie hurried over to take hold of stinging hands she'd foolishly forgotten to protect. "Why, you shouldn't be running around in this heller of a storm!"

"I—I wanted to help," she managed, still breathing heavily.

"Well, that's mighty good of you." Cookie smiled, rubbing life back into her cold fingers. "Me and Archie could use another pair of hands, truth be told. But I don't know if Mr. Beau'd want his guest workin'."

Amy smiled and removed her fingers from the compassionate woman's ministrations. "I'm sure he'd expect me to help." Numbly, she fumbled to untie her hood. Her fingers tingled painfully and so did her cheeks and nose. She wasn't used to the sort of cold Wyoming could dish out, and decided she'd better take more care to bundle up from now on. This kind of cold could kill very quickly. "What—what do you want me to do?"

"Maybe make us another big pot of strong coffee?" Cookie suggested.

"How strong?" Amy followed the older woman to the kitchen area, where a big, stainless-steel urn stood in a corner, emitting fragrant steam.

Cookie laughed. "That's easy. Just make it strong enough to haul a broke-down pickup, hon, and it'll be dandy."

Amy nodded, unsure how strong that might be, but deciding it was probably a million times stronger than she'd ever *considered* making coffee. "Tow-truck strength it is." She headed for the coffee urn, determined not to mess up her first emergency assignment. They might have to eat it with a fork, but if nothing else, her coffee would be *strong*.

The hours blurred. If she wasn't shoveling coffee into the urn, she was slicing beef or smearing bread with mustard, piling on lettuce, pickles, cheese, or washing ton after ton of dishes, as the cowboys took shifts breaking ice and feeding the three thousand head of cattle that were wintering there.

She'd overheard a couple of the hands talking about ten young cows that were having babies during the blizzard—calving, they'd called it. Even though they were in the relative warmth of the barn, she had a feeling this wasn't the most ideal night for little baby cows to come into the world. She wished the little guys and their mommies luck. She supposed cows were no luckier than humans when it came to timing a baby's birth. Didn't it always seem like babies were born in the worst possible circumstances? In taxis or storms or theater lobbies?

She didn't have time to dwell on the miracle of birth happening nearby. She had cold, hungry men to feed. Hours ago, she'd slipped into her cocktail-waitress mentality and was moving automatically amid the chaos and noise, smiling, serving, cleaning up, smiling, serving.

Along about dawn, she laid a plate loaded down with two roast beef sandwiches and a mound of barbecued beans before yet another cowboy. Noticing the pitcher of cream was empty, she reached across to pick it up, intent on refilling it, but felt a hand grip her wrist. "What the hell are you doing?" came her host's accusatory voice.

She stared down into critical eyes, startled to discover she'd just served Beau without realizing it. She must be more woozy from lack of sleep than she'd thought. Had it only been last night when he'd ambled into her bathroom, humiliated her beyond repair, then grabbed up some gloves and promptly forgotten about her? So much for her fears of how she'd ever face him again. He was his old, disagreeable self.

She jerked from his grasp. "I'm dancing *Swan Lake*! What does it look like I'm doing?" Startled to hear herself so uncharacteristically snappish, she sighed wearily. "I'm sorry. I guess I'm just tired. Do you want coffee?"

His eyes narrowed, and he continued to watch her for another few seconds. She noticed he looked fatigued around his eyes, his hair was wet and mussed and his striking features were snowburned. She swallowed at the sight. He and his men were fighting a rough battle against blinding, freezing elements she'd only spent a few seconds struggling against. What must they be suffering in an effort to save their cattle? Against her better judgment, her heart went out to him. She was about to wish him luck when he nodded curtly in answer to her question about coffee, then, without further comment, lowered his gaze to his plate to continue eating.

Aware that she'd been summarily dismissed, she spun away, her ire sparking again. "You're welcome, Mr. Diablo. Happy to help!" she grumbled, heading for the coffee urn.

She was tired, but not so tired that she didn't notice Beau leaving in a billow of windblown snow. She hadn't realized she'd stopped what she was doing until the cowman, Ed, touched her arm. "Miss Amy," he asked tentatively, "is them sandwiches for me?"

She snapped back to reality, grinned down at him and handed him his refilled plate. "Coffee coming up," she said as cheerfully as she could, then spun away to refill his mug.

The blizzard raged on and on, abusing the little cook house from all sides as wind-driven snow swirled and ranted and shrieked outside. Amy was accustomed to the cook-house door opening and closing every fifteen minutes or so with a new batch of ravenous, snow-covered cowhands coming and going. But when the door suddenly burst wide open with an explosive bang, she lurched around in shock and fear, almost depositing a pile of hot barbecued beans in Marv's lap. The cowhand caught the tipping plate, but Amy hardly noticed as Beau surged into the room, a bandanna covering his nose and mouth and his coat collar turned up. He looked like an Old West bandit, and Amy's pulse accelerated against her will. He was loaded down with a large bundle clutched in his arms, a couple of gangly brown legs and hoofed feet protruding from the horse blanket he carried.

As she stared, he stalked to the fireplace and spread the blanket over the oval rag rug, displaying a spindling newborn calf, all brown with a precious white face and the biggest black eyes. The poor little thing seemed so weak it was barely able to lift its head. "We need to warm this one up," Beau shouted, yanking down his bandanna. *"Cookie!"* he called.

"Boss, it'll be a minute." She held up flour-coated hands. "I'm in the middle of a batch of biscuits."

Amy was standing a few feet from where Beau was kneeling and rubbing the calf with a gloved hand. Setting the plate in front of Marv, she turned toward the sickly animal sprawled before the fire, and her heart twisted with concern. "I—can I help?" Having always lived in apartments in the city, she'd never even owned a dog, so she wasn't sure what to do with a sick calf. But it looked so pitiful and sweet, with those big, sorrowful eyes aimed her way. She had to do something.

She was on her knees beside the shivering calf before Beau had time to respond. When she placed a hand on the baby's thin rib cage and began to mimic Beau's stroking movements, she could hear him shift to look at her. For a minute, she didn't look back, just continued to stroke along the calf's silky, damp fur. "Like this?" When he didn't immediately answer, she reluctantly met his gaze.

His glare drilled through her. "What the hell sort of game are you playing, Miss Vale?"

Hurt by his continued antagonism, she grew defiant. "It's obviously too alien an idea for you to grasp, Mr. Diablo. But just so you'll recognize it in the future, it's called *trying to help*. Now, am I doing this right or not?"

They stared at each other, the sparks of their mutual hostility almost visible in the air around them. A weak bawling sound brought them back, and Beau snapped his attention away to look at the calf, automatically patting it. When his hand brushed hers, Amy drew away from his touch, but continued to stroke the shivery animal.

"Try to get her to take some milk." He retrieved a baby bottle from beneath his coat and thrust it toward her. "I'll be back in a couple of hours to check on her." When she took the bottle, he stood, half pivoted away, then stopped.

Amy looked up at him, prepared for another outburst of bad temper. When she met his eyes, she was startled to see something else mingled with the antipathy glimmering there. What was it? Guarded civility? Possibly even gratitude? His jaw shifted from side to side, and his nostrils flared. She stiffened, waiting, but for what she didn't know.

Yanking off his hat, he dragged a hand through his hair and spun to leave. As he did, she thought she heard him mutter something. Whatever it had been, it was more growled than spoken, but she was almost sure he'd uttered one small but significant word—*Thanks*.

She stared after him as he tromped off and swung open the door, exiting in a riot of storm-tossed snow.

Bewildered, she shifted back to her trembly charge. Scooting closer, she supported its wobbly head in her lap. "Did he really say that, little one?" She rubbed its scrawny neck. "Or am I so exhausted I'm having fits of delirium?"

Amy felt warm and cozy, except for a little crick in her neck. The bed seemed hard, and her pillow was missing. But she was so tired she didn't mind. It was nice just getting the chance to sleep.

She heard an odd shushing sound, then a scrape of wood against wood, followed quickly by what sounded like a masculine murmur. She stretched and sighed. Probably just the wind—the everlasting, pummeling blizzard.

A cough registered in her sleep-hazed brain. *Wind didn't cough, did it*? She stirred again, her eyes fluttering open a crack. She saw what seemed like the flicker of firelight, then closed her eyes. It was so toasty and welcome against her face she didn't want to wake up and find it was only a dream. She turned slightly, her hand coming to rest on something furry— and moving? She slid her fingers over it, perplexed. Why did her sheets feel as if they were covered in hair—and breathing?

Her eyes came wide open, and she looked around, hoping she was wrong about where she was. Unfortunately, the first thing her glance came to rest on was a pair of familiar black cowboy boots. Her glance surged up to take in the man lounging not far away at the cook-house table.

She swallowed, forcing her gaze upward to his face, indistinct beneath the wide brim of a cowboy hat. Even though she couldn't see his features well, she had a terrible feeling a pair of hypercritical eyes were trained on her.

"Good morning, Miss Vale," Beau drawled, pushing the wide brim back with his thumb. "Sleep well?" She could see his face now and was startled to note that he was less grim than she'd imagined he would be. But she wasn't relieved, for what she did see was worse. His eyes held the glitter of wry amusement. No doubt he found her inability to keep up during a blizzard highly satisfying. He seemed to be silently saying "I told you so," and that hurt! *The superior bum*! But she had to admit, she *had* failed— even in her own eyes. Abashed, she lowered her perusal to the sleeping calf and nervously stroked its rib cage.

She heard a few throats being cleared and her gaze flew back up. For the first time, she became aware that most of the cowhands were gathered around the long table, quietly eating. Apparently they'd tried to be quiet in deference to their sleeping guest.

Feeling like a complete fool, she struggled to sit, drawing a drowsy moo from her sleepy charge, its head still nestled in her lap. "What time is it?" she asked, brushing a stray wisp of hair from her face.

"Around ten. Blizzard's letting up." Cookie hurried over with a mug of steaming coffee. "You ought to go back to bed, hon. Archie and me can handle things from here on."

She gratefully took the mug and sipped, grimacing at the bitter taste. "No—no, I'm fine," she lied.

"The calf doing okay?" Beau queried, even though he was fully aware that Amy's attention had not been riveted on the animal lately.

Her cheeks went fiery at his continued taunting, but she worked at ignoring it. "Well—she had a couple of bottles of milk after she quit shivering. Then she settled down and slept." Unable to meet his gaze, she asked, "Doesn't she look better to you?"

He got up from the bench to kneel beside her. "I think she can go back to her mother now."

He gathered the blanket around the calf, but when he began to lift her, Amy put a restraining hand on his arm. "Are you sure that's a good idea?"

He looked at her, then at her hand resting on his arm. When he looked back, his features had eased into a contrary grin. "I'm fairly sure it's a good idea, Miss Vale, even though I've only had thirty-five years of ranching experience."

She didn't doubt that he knew his business, but she couldn't help the way she felt. She'd bonded with this little creature and was unhappy with the idea of it going out in such bitter cold. "What if she gets chilled?"

"Her mother can take care of her now."

Amy frowned as he lifted the baby in his arms. "You're not going to kill her and eat her, are you?"

He shifted to stare at her, his brows knitting. "You're going to make a *fine* rancher's wife."

"Are you?"

He shrugged, readjusting his bundle, its big black eyes on her. "She'll grow up and have babies of her own, Miss Vale. Feel better?"

She inhaled deeply, surprised she'd been holding her breath. Scrambling up, she patted the calf between its eyes. "See you later, Desiree," she whispered.

"Desiree?" Beau echoed incredulously.

"I named her that." She squared her shoulders mutinously. "She looks like a Desiree to me. What does she look like to you?"

"Pretty much like a cow."

There were a couple of snickers from his men. "I think she looks like a Desiree, boss," Ed piped up.

"Heck, yeah," Marv interjected. "If I said it once today, I said it a thousand times. Now that little heifer is a *Desiree* if I ever seen one!"

Beau frowned at his men. "You're all very funny. Maybe you should give up ranching and go on the comedy-club circuit."

Laughter abounded and Amy blinked in surprise. She looked back and forth from Beau to his men, surprised to discover that they liked him well enough to kid with him. Oddly, he didn't seem upset. His lips quirked in what looked very much like the beginnings of a grin. "Bye, *Desiree,* sweetheart," she ventured cautiously, offering a small smile as she stroked its soft forehead. "I'll come visit you."

As if in answer, the cow gave out a loud bawl and licked her hand.

"Lord," Beau muttered, turning to go amid wry calls from his cowhands of "So long, Desiree" and "Keep warm, little Desiree."

Amy couldn't stifle a giggle. For once, he was on the receiving end of the teasing, and she was tickled to witness it.

Even amid the jovial chatter, she had a feeling he heard her laugh, for at the door he paused. His gaze veered her way, and she froze, stunned and more disconcerted now than she'd been since she first met Beau Diablo. She thought he would stare daggers at her, but he didn't. His striking blue eyes held the flicker of grudging humor, and somehow, that disturbed her more than his fury ever had.

*   *   *

Wyoming was a white wonderland to Amy. Every-thing was half-buried in snowdrifts three to five feet deep, and trenches crisscrossed the land where cow-hands on horseback trekked from buildings to barns to equipment sheds to pastures, and where they con-tinuously had to break up ice on the creek and ponds and feed and doctor the cattle.

She'd grabbed a quick shower, but was back in the cook house in time to help Cookie and Archie serve beef stew and biscuits for lunch. Now, she was sitting in the back of a sleigh wagon full of hay bales, snow falling gently around her. The two husky horses drawing the wagon were high-stepping through the snow, huffing and puffing clouds of white in the frigid, overcast afternoon.

Ed was driving the team and Marv was nearby, cutting wire from around the bales in preparation for distributing the hay when they reached the low pasture where hungry cattle lowed and loitered.

The wagon topped a rise and she could see the cattle. Hundreds and hundreds roamed the valley, some tan, some black, some white with blotches of brown. Sitting tall in the saddle, roaming among them, she spied the unmistakable form of Beau Diablo. He was motioning, shouting orders to his men, but he was too far away for Amy to distinguish what he was saying.

She turned to Marv, the bearded bear of a man who spoke rarely, but when he did, it was bound to be witty. "Marv," she asked, drawing his squinty gaze, "what are they doing?" She gestured toward Beau.

Marv shifted his ceaseless squint toward his boss just as Beau began to spin a rope above his head. Before Amy could register what was happening, he'd

dropped the lasso over a nearby steer. The animal
didn't seem thrilled at being roped around the neck,
and tried to scamper away. As he kicked and struggled,
another cowboy lassoed his hind legs and yanked,
toppling the cow on its side. As it fell, Beau dis-
mounted and ran to the squirming beast. A third
cowhand joined his boss, holding the cow still.

"He's playin' doctor today, ma'am." Making a
pained face, Marv shook his shaggy head. "I can't
stomach watchin' him stick them cows with a needle.
Passed clean out a couple of times. So I get hayin'
duty. Which is fine by me."

Amy watched as Beau kneeled beside the steer's
rump. Though he was too far away for her to discern
details, she could tell by his movements that he was
giving the poor thing a shot. "Why's he doing it?"
she asked, feeling queasy.

"That yearling's got pinkeye. After the boss sticks
it, he'll spray his bad eye with medicine. Leastways
that's what I hear. Never seen it myself, 'cause once
I see that needle, I'm suckin' sod."

Amy swallowed spasmodically. She glanced away,
noticing the man still in his saddle was straining on
his rope, working to keep the animal immobile. After
a minute, Beau moved to the cow's head and treated
the infected eye with an aerosol spray. The cowboy
who had been holding the steer stroked its exposed
side with some kind of stick. "What's he doing now?"

"Paint stick," Marv explained minimally. "Ol'
Homer paints 'em with the date, so the boss knows
when that steer's been doctored and can check it in
a couple of days."

"Oh..." Amy wondered if giving cows shots would
become part of her job one day. She didn't like shots

much, and cringed at the idea that she'd humiliate herself by ending up fainting, too. Trying to quell a growing discomfort in her stomach, she took a couple of deep breaths. Her gaze drifted back to Beau as he retrieved his rope and pulled himself into his saddle with a masculine grace that bordered on criminal. Turning abruptly away from the stimulating sight, she called to Ed, "Uh—let me know when to start forking this stuff out to them."

He leaned around to smile at her, his droopy mustache frosty and stiff. "You sure you don't want to drive the team, Miss Amy? Me and Marv can pitch the hay."

She smiled back. "I'd drive us into a tree."

"I could teach you real quick," he offered, his Adam's apple bobbing nervously.

Amy sensed that he had a bit of a crush on her. Though he was trying to hide it, he wasn't doing very well. Not wanting to encourage him, she shook her head. "Maybe someday after I get *really* good at haying—"

"Your optimism is admirable, Miss Vale."

Amy jerked around to find Beau astride his black stallion, trotting up behind them. Surprised by his relatively pleasant response, she said, "Why— thanks."

He grinned, a dashing, crooked show of teeth that brought out a roguish dimple in one cheek. She had no idea why, but the out-of-character charm sent a tingle of unease along her spine. "On the other hand," he drawled, "it's been said that an optimist is someone who hasn't had enough experience."

That did it! She'd taken all the ridicule from this man she could stand. Bristling, she cried, "I'd rather be an optimistic *fool* than an arrogant tyrant!'' Her anger drove her to her feet. ''I've tried to think well of you, Mr. Diablo, but I've had enough of your disapproving attitude. As far as I'm concerned, you're a bitter, suspicious man, and I feel sorry for you!''

Without having to look, she knew Ed and Marv were staring in horror. The wagon had stopped, and it seemed as though the whole world had gone starkly silent. She hadn't known her host long, but one thing she was sure of. Beau Diablo was not a man who allowed himself to be insulted in public and then granted pardon easily. She had a feeling that if the roads weren't still closed west of them, she'd soon be standing waist-deep in snow, thumbing a ride to Diablo Butte. From the glower on his face, she had a sinking feeling she might be anyway, closed roads or no closed roads.

His jaw worked for what seemed like an eternity. It was agonizingly clear he was reining in his temper and finding the job difficult. ''Marv!'' He shifted his sparking gaze to the bearded cowboy squatting motionless amid the bales. ''You and Ed finish the haying. I'm shorthanded at the creek. I thought Miss Vale could help over there.'' Urging his mount up beside the wagon, he held out a hand to her. ''Slip onto the saddle in front of me. It's too far to walk.''

Now it was Amy's turn to stare in horror. She had no intention—no desire whatsoever—to be *that* close to him. Besides, she'd never ridden a horse in her life. ''On—on that?'' she squeaked.

''I'm fresh out of sports cars at the moment.'' He lifted a sardonic brow. ''The *best* rancher's wife in Wyoming would be able to ride a horse.''

That was a dare if she'd ever heard one. She could tell from the steely hardness of his eyes that he'd like nothing better than to have her decline, admit she couldn't take it. She'd be *darned* if she'd give him the satisfaction.

Even as determined as she was, she hesitated. There was no room on the saddle for her. She'd be in his *lap*! "But—but I won't be riding the horse, I'll be riding—" She clamped her lips closed, avoiding his eyes. More quietly, she asked, "Couldn't I please have my own horse?"

His exhale was born of aggravation. "The cattle don't have time for you to indulge in a charade of modesty, Miss Vale. We have work to do."

She hated to admit it, but he was right. It would take an hour for him to go back to the ranch headquarters and get her a horse. And she couldn't plod around in three feet of snow for very long without dropping out of sight from exhaustion and freezing to death—since he'd eat his fancy boots before he'd send out a search party.

Reluctantly handing her pitchfork to Marv, she took hold of the wagon's rail and lifted one boot over the edge. The black stallion whinnied, but was otherwise very still. She was grateful for that, but paused, not quite sure how to go about settling onto Beau's thighs. It wasn't so much that she wasn't sure how to do it; gravity would take care of getting on. It was more that she was trying to figure out how to best do it without *touching* him.

"Dammit, I'm not a nest of rattlesnakes." She felt herself being grasped by the waist and set squarely on his hard thighs. She didn't know if it was the landing

or the unsettling location, but her breath caught in
her chest and she couldn't speak.

They'd traveled some distance from the wagon when
she found her voice, but she didn't know what to say.
Hysteria was bubbling up inside her, and she had to
fight an urge to burst into tears. Whether her
emotional turmoil was because of pure exhaustion,
Beau's incessant rudeness or his unwelcome intimacy,
she couldn't fathom.

She knew she'd overreacted back on the wagon. She
knew she was overreacting now. But knowing it didn't
seem to help, not with Beau's thighs warm against her
hips, making her crazy. And *that* realization made her
angry. She didn't know if she was angrier at herself
or at him. She couldn't think straight. Whatever it
was, she simply couldn't stop herself from hissing,
"I've met a lot of jerks in my work, but I've never
met a man I despised so completely as I despise you!"

A chuckle near her ear astounded her. After that
outburst, she'd expected him to toss her into a
snowbank and leave her to be devoured by buzzards
after the spring thaw. "Well, well," he whispered.
"Maybe it would do you good to work off some of
that healthy hatred wielding a sledgehammer."

She sagged with defeat. What was with this man?
It was almost as if he was *trying* to make her hate
him, pushing her away with taunts and sarcasm. She
had no idea why anyone would deliberately do such
a thing, but if that was Beau's aim, he was succeeding
beautifully. "You have a charming way of motivating
people, Mr. Diablo."

Another chuckle rumbled through her as his exhilarating aroma invaded her senses. Blanching, she
clutched the saddle horn, leaning as far away from

his chest as possible. Unfortunately, there was no escaping the manly feel of him beneath her as they bounced through the snowy meadow. It mortified her to discover how stirring his closeness was, even now, after she'd made it very clear she felt *nothing* for him but contempt.

CHAPTER FIVE

CAPTIVITY in Beau's arms was a disconcerting experience. She'd been so cold for so long, she found his radiating warmth to be every bit as inviting as his attitude was offensive. She bit the inside of her cheek, frustrated by her warring emotions. Cuddled there, his hands on the reins only inches from her breasts, his warm breath caressing her cheek, she was having difficulty keeping her loathing for him worked up to a frenzy.

He projected an energy, an exotic power that drew her against her will. She'd never experienced anything like it before with any man. Even when he was growling at her, her pulse raced and her throat went dry. She didn't like the helplessness of the feeling his nearness caused, didn't like the way he derailed her logical thinking and made her mind careen down disgraceful paths.

"Have you spoken with Ira today?" he murmured near her ear.

"*Who*?" She jumped, trying to gather her wayward thoughts.

"Ira?" he coaxed. "Your fiancé and my father?" Readjusting the reins, he brushed her breast with his arm. Even through her parka, she registered the touch and her flesh tingled. Pulling her lips between her teeth, she inhaled to calm herself. Seconds ticked by, long seconds, but she couldn't find her voice.

"Would you like to start with a simpler question?"

76

She winced at his sarcasm. "The phone lines are down. I—I heard it on the radio when I went to my room to take a shower."

"I see."

Her heart hammered in her ears. What was her problem, and why did he seem to have the power to reduce her to acting like a complete dolt? This couldn't go on. *She had to get out of here.* "When do you think the roads will be clear?" she asked, upset by the frantic edge in her voice.

"Around here, they'll be bulldozed by tonight."

"Then I should be able to get to Diablo Butte tonight?"

"I said, around here." He gave his stallion a signal with his legs and his muscles flexed seductively beneath her. It was all she could do to keep from screaming. "High winds through Diablo Pass will prevent the dozers from clearing the road for another day or two. That is, *if* we don't get more bad weather."

"Oh—no..."

Another bothersome chuckle sent a shiver through her, and it startled her to discover she was leaning against him. When had that happened?

"I'd love to sit here and bask in your enthusiasm, Miss Vale, but we're here." Before the words were out of his mouth, he'd somehow managed to dismount, leaving her in his saddle. "Grab my shoulders." He lifted his arms to help her down.

"Grab your *own* shoulders." She swung her leg over the saddle horn to the opposite side, intent on dismounting as far away from him as possible. She slid to the ground, delighted with herself for her smooth escape. Unfortunately, the soft snow was deeper than she'd anticipated, and she couldn't find her footing.

With a surprised squeal, she sprawled face first in the pillowy drift.

Beau's stallion snorted and pranced with surprise, and she wondered if her rashness was about to get her trampled to death. As quickly as she could, she rolled away, clearing snow from her eyes. When she righted herself, the first sight she saw was Beau, towering above her, his lips quirked in wry amusement.

"Okay, go ahead," she charged. "Tell me the best rancher's wife in Wyoming would have been able to get *more* snow down her blouse!"

Lifting a brow, he warned softly, "Don't do that again, Miss Vale." He affectionately stroked his stallion's neck. "Not many horses take surprises as well as Sovereign."

She grew fidgety under his close observation and dropped her glance to the spot where the big stallion was pawing impatiently at the snow. She couldn't think of a single argument in her defense. Probably because she had none.

"Want a hand up?"

"*No!*" She shoved against the snow in an attempt to stand, but once again couldn't find a solid hold. Her arm sank deeper, and she plummeted back downward, tasting snow again. "Don't you—*dare* say anything!" she sputtered.

She found herself being lifted. While she cleared her vision, she was carried several strides away. About the time she could see, he said, "Empty your mind, Miss Vale. Try to visualize standing upright."

She glared at him. "You're so cute!"

"People will say we're in love." His tormenting grin made her senses leap foolishly. Before she could think of a sharp retort, he dumped her unceremoniously on her feet. This time, she managed to remain standing, for he'd deposited her in an area beneath a tree where the snow had been trampled by his men. He indicated an ax and a sledgehammer leaning against the cottonwood trunk. "If you're not too exhausted from your little Indiana Jones quest to stand up, go take J.C.'s place chopping ice. Tell him to use the snowmobile and scout for broken fence and cattle that might have drifted during the storm."

Incensed at his belittling attitude, she stiffened. "Oh, right! Make *me* chop ice and let one of your big, strong hands ride around in a snowmobile." She fairly shivered with rage. "Some people would say that's not a wise use of manpower."

Irritation flickered across his face. "How many of your ribs are cracked?"

She blinked, startled by the question. "Uh—why—none."

"I see. Well, J.C. has three cracked ribs, and he's hurting, but he won't admit it and he won't take any time off." She was taken aback and must have looked it, for he chuckled ruefully. "From your expression I assume you haven't nominated me for sainthood." He crossed his arms at his chest. "No matter what you think, Miss Vale, everyone has some good traits. Even me. I assume you have some, too."

That remark tweaked her pride. "But so far you haven't seen *any*?" she demanded.

He didn't respond immediately, merely watched her. After a strained silence, his lips twisted ruefully. "I'll give you credit for one thing. You take more punishment than I thought you would."

She eyed him with pure abhorrence. "Your sentiment is so enchanting I think I'll have it embroidered on a pillow!"

The squeak of leather was her only answer as he mounted his stallion.

Upset that he could remain so dispassionate while forcing her to the brink of hysteria, she said, "For your information, I'll relieve J.C. and I'll break up your darned ice as well as any man."

He'd nudged Sovereign into a turn, but when she spoke, he halted his mount and looked at her, his expression preoccupied. "Did you say something?"

Wanting to get a rise out of him and not sure why such a crazy need was so strong in her, she lied, "I said your name suits you, Mr. *Diablo*. I'm sure you'd be right at home in Hades!"

Though his flexing jaw told her she'd hit a nerve, she didn't feel vindicated. As she stared up at him, an emotion more distressing than anger held her in its grip. He was an imposing, self-confident presence on his big stallion. His magnetism was riveting, almost overpowering. She'd intended to spin disdainfully away, but faced with his lean good looks and his hooded stare, she had to compel herself to break eye contact. Her spin, when she finally made it, was more regretful than adamant.

Unclenching a fist she had no idea she'd clenched, she grabbed for the sledgehammer. It made her stumble when it didn't budge. She hadn't realized how heavy a sledgehammer was.

"It appears your hatred of me isn't as strong as you thought, Miss Vale," he taunted. "I'd work on it. Meanwhile, use the ax."

Before she could spin around and suggest that he might rethink giving deadly weapons to women who despised him, she heard the muffled sound of hooves plowing through deep snow as Beau spurred his stallion back to work.

Amy was surprised at how warm she was. Even though the wind had picked up and the pewter sky was spitting new snow, she wasn't cold. The exercise of slamming an ax into ice for the past hour had kept her blood flowing all the way to the tips of her fingers. But warm or not, her muscles were crying out that they were going to stop functioning altogether if she didn't take a break.

"Miss Amy? Want some coffee?"

She shifted toward the young cowboy about her age, called Snapper. His face was long and bony and red from the cold. An unlit cigarette hung from a corner of his wide mouth because, as he'd told her, he was trying to quit but couldn't give up the feel of it dangling there.

She straightened from her crouched position, grateful for the respite. She accepted the thermos lid with a smile. "Thanks, Snapper." Now she understood why coffee out here was so strong. The caffeine kept these men pumped up with the energy they needed for the intense cold and physical labor. In her case, it was keeping her awake after days of little or no sleep.

"Take a breather, Miss Amy," he said. "This is mighty hard work, especially for a city gal."

She took a sip of the strong brew, beginning to wonder if her mind was that easy to read. Still, she didn't dare take a rest. All she needed was to have

Beau ride up and find her sitting around doing nothing.

"See, the rule is," Snapper went on, "fifteen minutes off every hour. Ain't it, Willie?"

The fortyish wrangler with a scar where his right eye should be and a graying braid hanging to his waist, stopped shoveling ice. Leaning on the shovel handle, he nodded. "You betcha, ma'am." He winked his good eye. "Take your time with that java. Have yourself another cup. Me and Snapper'll be fine."

She sighed, unable to deny she needed a rest. Taking another sip, she nodded her thanks and set her ax down near the thermos and Snapper's sledgehammer. "I think I will."

"Take a good, long spell." Snapper hefted the sledge. "You done your share and more already."

She savored another taste of the hot coffee and scanned the creek where they'd already broken the surface ice. Cattle contentedly lapped at the water, oblivious to the fact that they were being waited on hand and foot. She shook her head, murmuring toward the cattle, "A thank-you would be nice, guys."

She grinned and turned to examine the frozen stream as it undulated along the draw. About fifty feet on down, it disappeared into a lush thicket. How lovely. There was a quaint little fence made from branches on this side of the thicket. It didn't seem to be holding anything, had no gate. It was just a little circle of fence about ten feet across, curving along the landscape. Snow mantled and rustic, it made a tranquil scene.

She wished she had a camera. Every direction she faced, she was confronted by a fantasyland of snow, juxtaposed against the stark beauty of denuded limbs, twisted trunks and dramatic rock outcroppings. Or she would delight in the grace of scampering jackrabbits, spy a shy deer peeping at her from a copse of pines, or gasp at the majesty of big horned elk off in the distance, silhouetted against sparkling whiteness. There was so much untamed, unpretentious beauty here. Every day, almost hourly, she found this dazzling wilderness more and more thrilling. After experiencing Wyoming in winter, she knew she could never be contented in a big city again.

"Miss Vale! *Stop!*"

Amy almost spilled her coffee when she heard Beau's stern command, and she gritted her teeth with consternation. He *would* show up just when she was taking her break. She'd reached the little fence and bent to step through the rails. As she did, she turned and shouted, "I don't take well to intimidation, Mr. Diablo!"

"Come back here!"

"*Make me,* Mr. Big Shot!" After stepping through the fence, she straightened and trudged away, vowing to ignore him. There was a nice-size rock on the far side of the little pen where she could sit and lean against the fence to finish her coffee. Beau Diablo had no right to shout at her and treat her like a two-year-old. She'd been *told* she could take a break and she planned take it. If he wanted to browbeat her, he could just wait until she finished her coffee.

"Dammit! *Amy!*"

Her first clue that anything was wrong was when she watched the thermos lid go flying into the air, tumbling end over end as it flung its dark contents to the wind. Before she could imagine what caused it, she was jerked backward as something cinched her around the waist. It was as though a sea monster had reached out with a tentacle and snatched her off her feet. The only problem with that scenario was that she wasn't twenty thousand leagues under the sea. She stumbled once, but finally lost her battle with gravity and fell with a cry.

As soon as she was sprawled on her back, she came up flailing defensively. She focused her struggles on the tentacle gripping her waist, fearful she'd become the captive of some sort of Wyoming killer snow snake intent on squeezing the life out of her. But when she saw what clutched her, she was astounded to discover it was nothing more lethal than a length of rope.

Rope? Her mind was so clouded by fear it took her a second or two for that fact to register. But when it did, she grew livid. Rope? As in *lasso*?

"Beau Diablo!" she growled. "You did this, you controlling *swine*!" How dare he use physical force to get his way. It was then that she noticed the sound of horses' hooves thundering her way and she scrambled around, struggling to stand. She grappled to free herself, but Beau was keeping the rope taut and she found herself yanked against the fence. To keep from tumbling over it, she clamped her hands on the wood and glared at him. He was walking his stallion now, gathering his rope as he came, leaving her no slack.

She threw him a reproachful glare. "Who do you think you are, the Sundance Kid? I'm going to—I hope you know I plan to—" She swallowed, so furious she couldn't think of a threat horrible enough to fling at him. She tried again. "You—you bullying snake! I—I—*Don't come near me!*"

He climbed down from his horse and continued to imprison her against the fence while he looped the excess rope in his other hand. When he reached the fence, he startled her by straddling it and stepping over. He was only inches away now, and she couldn't escape him.

He said her name but she cut him off. "Let me go!" Punctuating her demand, she pummeled his chest. "I'm going to have you arrested for kidnapping and—and mugging and—and—illegal use of a *lasso*, and—"

"Amy!" He took her by the arms and gave her a shake. "Shut up."

"I won't shut up! I—I..." She frowned when he shifted toward the fence. Incensed that he would ignore her in the face of her fury, her glower followed his movements to find out what he was up to. "What are you doing? Why are you tying me to the fence?"

"So you can't get into any more trouble." He yanked the knot tight. "Now, be still and watch."

She yanked on the rope, but when it didn't give, she twirled toward him, intent on giving him another piece of her mind. Though she'd opened her mouth to shout at him, she stopped before any more recriminations could tumble out. As she glared, he kicked aside some snow and located a boulder about the size of a bowling ball and picked it up. She stared, perplexed. What was he planning to do? "Do you intend to hit me with that?"

"It's a thought," he grumbled without turning her way. "You'd be less trouble unconscious." He tossed the heavy rock about two feet in front of him, just beyond where she'd been before he'd jerked her back with his lasso.

To her surprise, the rock promptly disappeared. When it did, the disturbed snow around the hole also began to fall away a chunk at a time. The thermos lid toppled sideways and dropped out of sight. After a few seconds, the hole had opened up to about three feet in diameter. Straining on the rope, she peered into the chasm. There was nothing but a black void beyond the snowy crust. "What—what is it?" she whispered.

"Sinkhole." He came to her and bent to untie her from the fence. "Next time, listen to me," he admonished softly.

She watched speechless as more snow lost its precarious grasp on the grasses that were bowed over the hole, disguising the crater from those who weren't aware of it.

"How—how deep is it?"

"Deep enough to break your neck."

When realization hit, she went weak and had to grab the rail to keep from sinking to her knees. "That's why there's a fence?"

As the rope went slack at her waist, his sultry tang invaded her senses, for he'd drawn very close to relieve her of her bonds. "That's why there's a fence," he repeated, lifting his gaze to hers.

When he did, their lips were barely a handsbreadth apart, his glorious blue eyes so close his lashes brushed her brow. She squeezed the railing, suddenly recklessly conscious of his sexual appeal. His stare was bold, lazily sensual, and she found herself battling an urge to move the short distance that separated them and press her lips to his. The idea jolted her, took her breath away.

She heard a muffled curse as Beau abruptly straightened. She wondered if something about the experience had bothered him, too, but didn't have the time to dwell on it, for he barked, "You can step out of the rope now, Miss Vale."

Something was wrong with her brain. She was moving in a drugged slow motion, and it took her several seconds to pull her gaze from his troubled eyes. With great effort, she managed to look down at her rubber boots. His lasso lay in a perfect circle in the snow. "Oh, right..." Before she moved, however, her glance lifted on its own to meet his again. What did she expect to see? What did she want to see? His eyes were shuttered now, giving away nothing.

In a self-protective impulse, she bent and stepped between the fence rails, putting distance between them. Supporting herself against the wood, she clutched her hands together. "Thank you, Mr. Diablo," she whispered, her eyes downcast, "for saving my life."

"You're welcome." There was movement as he crossed the fence. "And I'm sorry for the way I had to do that. I hope I didn't hurt you."

Not expecting an apology, she shifted toward him, but he was already gathering up his rope and heading toward his horse. "I'm okay—and I apologize, too." She hadn't been aware she was going to say that until the words were out of her mouth.

He was poised with one boot in the stirrup, but when she spoke he stopped, glancing at her. "For what?"

She shrugged, embarrassed. "For hitting you. I hope I didn't hurt you, either."

A faint sparkle lit his blue eyes. "I may never recover."

"And—and for the name-calling, too. I'm sorry—but—" she had to add in her defense "—you shout at me all the time, so how was I to know..." She let the sentence die.

"Good point," he acknowledged, going sober. "From now on, if I call you Amy, you're in danger. Deal?"

She nodded glumly. "You must have an interesting life, if every woman you call by her given name is in danger." He suddenly grinned, showing that slashing dimple in his cheek. Her heart turned over at the sight—so sexy yet at the same time so alarming. It belatedly occurred to her that her remark had another meaning, one she hadn't intended—that his female companions were in danger of succumbing to his masculine charisma. Heavens! Maybe he even mistakenly believed that *she* was affected that way. Her cheeks grew hot with mortification. "Wait a second. I hope you don't think—"

"Afternoon, Miss Vale," he drawled, cutting off her denial. With a finger to the brim of his hat, he bounded into his saddle and rode away.

She toyed with her lower lip as she headed back to Snapper and Willie and her ax. While she shuffled along, she began to have a nagging suspicion that Beau should have called her Amy when he'd smiled just then. Forcing the notion aside, she rebuked herself. *How foolish*! *What could be dangerous about a smile*?

Valentine's Day was passing swiftly. The roads west were still closed due to high winds and blowing snow, and the phone lines were still down for the same reason. Amy had spent the day just like she'd spent the previous two, and she felt pretty good about herself. She could break ice on a creek and toss hay from a pitchfork as well as any city-born-and-bred woman in America. At least any with three days' experience. Maybe she was grasping at straws for things to feel good about, but she had to try to feel positive about something. Today was supposed to have been her wedding day. Instead she was being worked like an indentured servant from dawn until dark in subzero temperatures by a glowering host.

At least there was one positive thing about today. She was going to get to experience a real live barn dance. Cookie had chattered happily about it as Amy had helped scramble eggs for breakfast. A neighboring rancher and his wife were celebrating their fiftieth wedding anniversary, and they were hosting an old-fashioned, down-home barn dance.

She smiled and patted Desiree's forehead. "So, I guess I'd better go, honey. You run back to your mama." Leaning through the fence of the pen behind the calving barn where the new calves were housed, she gave Desiree a hug. The cow bawled and nudged her cheek affectionately. "I love you, too. See you tomorrow."

Her bright mood faded with every step she took toward the ranch house. She hoped a barn dance would take her mind off her situation. Maybe, if she was lucky, Beau would be too busy to go. He hadn't left with the off-duty cowhands as they'd clambered into the newer pickup. The five wranglers who'd lost the draw to ride in the warm cab had crammed themselves into the truck bed along with insulated containers full of hot food. They hadn't seemed too unhappy with their fate, and had ridden away an hour ago, laughing and hooting, clearly planning to enjoy the distraction of an evening off.

She hadn't gotten far from the barn when she heard the jingling of bells. Pausing, she peered around to find the source of the sound. Out of the darkness, she spotted a pair of harnessed horses. They were drawing a wagon. No. As she looked closer, she could see it wasn't a wagon, but the most charming sleigh she'd ever seen. It was painted silver, its back seat and front seat made of red tufted leather.

She'd never seen a sleigh except in old romantic movies or on holiday greeting cards with Santa at the reins, but this had to be as charming as any she could imagine. Draped over the horses' backs were leather strips lined with silver bells, jingling and jangling as the horses pranced through the snow.

"Thought we'd come get you, Miss Amy," Archie called as he halted the team beside her.

He was sitting in the front seat. Cookie was in the back, a woolen lap blanket drawn up to her throat. "Slip that robe up there around your legs, hon," Cookie called. "It's gonna be about a forty-minute ride, so you'll welcome it before we get there."

Amy was so charmed by the idea of going on a sleigh ride, she didn't know what to say. Her spirits soared as she climbed up beside Archie and pulled the throw over her. She'd opted to wear a long, broomstick skirt tonight, and though she had on a slip, tights, lace-up boots and heavy socks, the throw was going to help. "This is exciting!" She shifted to smile at Cookie. "I thought we were going in the old truck."

"That old sweetheart's been dying on me the past couple of days." Archie shook his head, the tassel of his red wool cap bobbing to and fro. "Since we had this little rig in the machine shed, I decided why not use her. There's nothing in this world as dependable as *real* horsepower."

Amy sat back, breathing in the crisp night air. "Oh, it's just so wonderful. I never imagined—"

"What the *hell* is this?"

Amy jerked up, startled to hear Beau's irritated question. She could just make him out, stalking toward them from the direction of the ranch house.

"Howdy, boss." Archie waved, seemingly unconcerned by the dire tone in Beau's voice. "I was jes' explainin' to Miss Amy about the pickup dyin' on me the past couple of days. Don't think we better chance it tonight. Could get stranded and that wouldn't be no fun."

Amy watched her host from beneath lowered lids. The floodlight above the barn door held him in its stark grasp, illuminating his wide-brimmed hat, his sternly sensual lips and the imposing width of his shoulders swathed in his split-cowhide coat. He stood not far away, his muscular legs braced wide. The tensing of his jaw betrayed high annoyance.

"Besides, boss," Cookie chimed in, "you know if we go cross-country we can cut twenty minutes off the trip. And we're late as it is."

Amy hoped the "we" she was talking about didn't include her host. Unfortunately, just as that hope sprang full bloom in her heart, Archie slid away from her. When she turned to see what he was doing, he'd already swung around to clamber into the back seat. "Hope you don't mind driving, Mr. Beau, but my bursitis is acting up on me in this cold."

Her hope died a silent, sickly death when Beau said nothing further. Scowling at his cook, he pulled himself up beside Amy and took the reins.

Cookie and Archie immediately became immersed in a lively discussion about how many years they'd been married. It had been going on all day and didn't sound as though it was near an end. "You're crazy, you old coot." Cookie laughed. "It'll be thirty-five years a week from today, and you know what the thirty-fifth anniversary gift is."

"Like I been tryin' to tell you, it ain't thirty-five, it's thirty-three. Do the math, old woman. Do the math."

As the couple behind them calculated aloud, chuckling and playfully grousing, Beau's thigh brushed hers and Amy swallowed hard. She shifted away as he signaled the team to move and they slid into motion. Amy remembered the lap blanket and knew she ought to do the polite thing. Nervously, she offered, "Uh—would you like a piece of my lap?"

Archie and Cookie continued to debate additions and subtractions at the top of their lungs as Beau canted his head in her direction. "Would I like a piece of your *lap*?" His gruffness seemed muted by curiosity. "Does this mean you care?"

She was horrified by her bizarre slip of the tongue. "Er—lap *blanket*!" She held up a corner of the wool for clarification. "I meant to say *blanket*."

"Did you?" His lips twisted as he held her gaze with shrewd, sparkling eyes. "Miss Vale, don't pretend you think, because you're engaged to my father, I wouldn't take you up on your proposition. We can share a blanket any time you say."

His challenge stunned her and she flung herself as far away from him as possible, which wasn't nearly far enough. "If I thought you *meant* that, Mr. Diablo, I'd slap your insolent face!" she warned under her breath. "For all I care, feel free to turn into Rudolph-the-red-nose *icicle*!"

CHAPTER SIX

THE Jones farm was all but hidden in a rugged, timbered valley. It was a quaint little spread out there in the middle of nowhere. The venerable barn looked like something out of an Old West movie. The first story was made of round pine logs while the top half was rough-sawn planks.

From atop the ridge where they were gliding along, Amy could see the front of the structure with its big double doors, bright light seeping out the cracks outlining it. Near the peak of the roof was a diamond-shaped window from which spilled more golden light. It was so picturesque she couldn't wait to get there—and leave a certain bothersome rancher's side.

Long before she'd been able to see any sign of civilization, she'd heard far-off Western music lilting across the frosty air. For most of the trip, the only sound she'd heard had been the jingling of bells on the horses' harness as they crunched through the sparkling, moonlit snow. Not long after they'd left the ranch, Cookie and Archie had lapsed into naps, and at the moment, neither was snoring. Beau, typically, had opted not to speak to her at all.

The melody wafting across the air was lively, and Amy found her foot tapping as she tried to recall the name of the piece the band was playing. It was a classic Western tune, but she couldn't quite think of the title.

She chanced a glimpse at Beau, silently handling the reins, leading the horses down into the valley. His expression was closed and he appeared to be concentrating on what he was doing as he led the team through the scattering of pines, heavy with twinkling snow.

She wondered if he noticed the beauty of the night or heard the far-off melody? Was he seeing the brightly lit barn? Did he detect the distant laughter that burst onto the night air every so often? On what dark trail did his thoughts dwell? She wondered, too, if he was cold. After his lewd remark earlier, she'd huddled alone in the blanket, trying to keep from noticeably shivering as the chill seeped through to her bones.

He didn't appear to be affected by the frigid temperature. She sighed, relatively sure she'd bitten off her own nose to spite her face. If she'd shared the lap blanket with him, she would be warmer now.

"What's that—s-song?" she asked, deciding since they were almost there, she might as well start getting into the spirit. Besides, talking would take her mind off freezing to death.

He turned his intense gaze on her. "Are you cold?"

Chafing beneath his regard, she wished she hadn't spoken at all. Defiantly, she shook her head. "I don't think that's the name of the tune. S-something about Texas, isn't it?"

His brows drew together in a fierce frown before he turned away. "It's 'Yellow Rose of Texas'," he muttered. "Miss Vale, if you were cold, you should have told me."

"Oh? What w-would you have done about it?"

"I would have kept you warm."

The quiet way he said it sent a quiver down her spine that had nothing to do with the weather. "I'd rather freeze," she retorted, hoping she meant it.

He considered her silently for a minute before he shifted away to guide the team to a protected area behind the barn where several other sleighs waited.

Amy compelled herself to take in the scene and to attempt to forget about Beau. She noticed a number of pickup trucks parked in the clearing before the barn, along with a half-dozen four-wheel-drive vehicles. There was a handful of saddled horses tied to a nearby hitching post, as well as a few snowmobiles scattered here and there. She shook her head, doubting she'd ever see this many different modes of transportation parked outside any Chicago party.

"The Yellow Rose of Texas" had ended and another tune began. Amy remembered hearing this one at the cowboy bar. It was something she liked by George Jones. She couldn't recall the name, and didn't intend to ask Beau. Hearing rustling behind her, she noticed that Cookie and Archie had awakened. "We here?" Cookie yawned loudly.

"Musta dropped off," Archie chimed in, sounding groggy.

Amy felt the sleigh bob and realized Beau had climbed down and was helping Cookie from the back. Gritting her teeth, she tossed the blanket aside and jumped down on her side. Intent on a swift escape, she took a step toward the barn, but found herself unable to move. She winced. Her skirt was caught on something, exposing most of her legs.

When she turned back to free herself, she caught Beau glancing her way.

"Problem?" he asked.

She couldn't see what her skirt was hooked on in the shadowy sleigh, but she had no plans to accept his help. "Nothing I can't handle." She fumbled in the darkness, but wasn't able to loosen her skirt from whatever was holding it.

"Sure?"

She cast him a defiant look. "I'm *fine.*"

With a dubious lift of his brow, he turned to help Archie lumber down.

"Better get on in, hon," Cookie called as she and her husband hustled toward a side door. "Cold out here."

"I'll—b-be right there." She smiled bravely, waving them off.

"Skirt caught?" came a soft question nearby.

Darn the man! She couldn't turn her back on him for one minute or he'd sneak up on her! "A little," she admitted. "But I have it under control." Unaccountably jittery, she tugged harder than she'd intended and couldn't miss the ripping noise.

"Sounds like it."

She exhaled, exasperated with herself for letting him get to her. She fumbled, but could hardly get her hands to work. It wasn't until then that she faced the fact that she was numb from the tip of her head to her toes. Her hands were like chunks of ice and her fingers would hardly obey her. The ripping noise came again.

Her fingers were brushed away and her skirt was abruptly freed from a loose nail. "You're welcome," he muttered, taking her arm and towing her toward the barn.

"I a-almost had it!"

"Out here, that's what we chisel on tombstones of the terminally stubborn."

She yanked on his hold. "Would you at least let me check my dress to see if I'm decent?"

"I'll do it."

She managed to free herself with one mighty jerk. "Oh, no, you won't!"

His eyes twinkled with such masculine appeal she couldn't find her voice for a minute. "But it's all in the family, isn't it—Mom?"

"That's *not* funny!" Flustered, she spun away to scrutinize her skirt, fearful of finding a bad rip.

"It's right there." He knelt to lift her hem. "You tore the bottom ruffle away for a couple of inches. Nobody will see it."

"Thank you, Calvin Klein!" She snatched the fabric from his hand and bent to inspect it. Sure enough, he was right. No real harm done. She could restitch it easily enough.

Hearing the squeak of hinges, she glanced up. Beau was holding the door for her.

"Coming?" he asked, once again his serious self.

"I suppose." She straightened and brushed at her skirt more from uneasiness than anything else.

"I'll introduce you around." Extending his arm, he wordlessly offered to escort her inside.

She brushed past him, carefully avoiding his touch. He didn't force the issue, just followed her in. Though she was unwilling to admit it, she supposed it was only right that Beau introduce her to her future neighbors. After all, he was Ira's son.

Pasting on a smile, she vowed to have a nice time, even though Beau Diablo would be under the same roof. That's why she didn't object when he helped her out of her parka and hung it on a harness peg. It was far harder to keep her pleasant facade when he took her arm and began guiding her from person to person, which was no easy task. The barn was one hundred feet by thirty, lined with stacks and stacks of hay bales that served as bleacher seats to accommodate the guests while they ate or rested from dancing.

For what seemed like an eternity, Beau helped her up and down, around and over bales and reclining people, introducing her to most everyone in the barn. Though she didn't think anyone else could tell, she was painfully aware that Beau's dashing grin was every bit as counterfeit as hers.

A deep, shadowy hayloft stretched across the back half of the barn. A number of people had clambered up to find spots to nap, smooch, clap along with the music, or simply get a better view of the dance floor, strewn with hay and clogged with high-spirited cowboys and their ladies. Along one side of the lower level was a row of stalls. No longer used for calving, they were now filled with coolers and boxes of extra food and drink. In front of the stalls stretched a row of tables heaped high with steaming barbecued ribs, potato salad, baked beans, pies, cakes, spiced apple cider, coffee and soft drinks. Near the back, a butane stove was putting out plenty of welcome heat.

On the other side of the barn, the band dominated on a platform made of hay bales and plywood. Between the two sides, couples two-stepped and waltzed around the floor, hooting and laughing, feet thudding in time-honored country rhythms on the worn pine floorboards. With the women outnumbered by the men, Amy had spent little time cooling her heels as a wallflower. She'd gotten to know every cowboy in the county almost as well as every crack and worn spot in the floor.

A few minutes ago, she'd declined several invitations to dance so she could take a breather. Perched on the end of a row of bales about halfway up the bleachers, she was enjoying her view of the dancefloor. She hadn't seen Beau for a while and assumed he was reacquainting himself with several of the local ladies—possibly up in a dark corner of the hayloft. It wasn't a particularly outlandish idea, considering how popular he seemed to be with the local women.

Unfortunately, even against her will, she'd taken notice of him from time to time on the dance floor as one pretty girl after another took a turn around the floor in his arms. But she *wasn't* counting and she *wasn't* watching and she *didn't* care where he was.

"Having fun?"

She almost shrieked with surprise, but stopped herself, wondering what was wrong with her nerves lately. Though she governed her features to remain unruffled, she couldn't quite meet his face. Instead she pretended to watch the dancers. "I don't know when I've had this much fun," she said truthfully, managing the beginnings of a real smile. "The cowboy bar can't hold a candle to this."

He didn't speak, and her curiosity made her turn toward him. When she did, she was startled to see that his face was very close to her own. She hadn't realized her elevated position would place her in such intimate proximity to eyes that were such a pure blue—unwavering and direct. Her smile faded, but she refreshed it quickly. "And—and everybody's nice, too."

"Yes, they are nice."

His lips were close. Too close. And even though his expression was serious, something in his eyes seemed far from dispassionate. "Would you like to dance?"

No! her mind cried. "I—yes..." She blanched. Who had said *that*?

As he took her hand and helped her down, she had the oddest feeling she was standing on the sidelines watching some idiot who bore a strong resemblance to herself slipping into Beau Diablo's arms. She wondered who the look-alike fool could be?

A new tune began, and Amy recognized it as one of the most popular requests at the cowboy bar. It was called "Shut Up and Kiss Me!" a lively, two-step. She was so startled when Beau pulled her against him, she stopped breathing. At the bar, she'd seen the really good two-steppers dance close like this. But if you weren't good at it, your legs could get tangled and you could trip your partner. Her heart thudded, with a vivid mental picture of herself toppling them both and ending up sprawled on the floor.

Why couldn't the band have opted to play the "Cotton-Eyed Joe"? Men didn't slide women into their embrace during the "Cotton-Eyed Joe". And she didn't need to be pressed against his hard torso the way she was, didn't need to feel his warm fingers splayed across the small of her back. She didn't need that at all.

"You're a good dancer," he murmured.

She met his eyes with difficulty. "Every once in a while, somebody in the bar would get drunk enough to pull me out onto the floor while I was trying to clean off a table. After four years, I've picked up most of the dances." She added honestly, "I'm surprised I can dance with somebody who's sober."

He grinned, displaying his bothersome dimple. "That explains why you stagger and weave more than most of my partners."

She giggled at his wit and was startled by her amused reaction. Quickly controlling herself, she lowered her gaze and found herself wanting to put distance between them—at least emotionally—since she was clasped so securely to his body. "It upset me a little that you introduced me to everyone as a family friend instead of Ira's fiancé."

He quirked a brow. "Not many people around here marry more than once, Miss Vale." Though he maintained his outward affability, there was a hardening in his tone. "Since you're to be Ira's fifth wife, let's just say I decided to spare you some embarrassment. At least for a while."

The cynicism of his remark grated on her. "That's very gallant of you, I'm sure."

"It's the least I could do as your host," he said, his tone equally caustic.

She wanted to slap his face and run away, but she endured the torture of his embrace, deciding it would be worse to make a scene. For a long time, they two-stepped around the floor without speaking, the lead singer whispering his husky "Shut up and kiss me!" all too often for Amy's state of mind.

She could feel the weight of Beau's gaze on her. When she could stand it no longer, she forced herself to meet it. His stare was insolent and assessing, but he didn't speak, didn't acknowledge the fact that she was staring at him, too. He merely held her against him, moving her expertly around the floor, watching her with that narrowed, penetrating look.

The long, silent observation preyed on her nerves, yet she was also filled with heady anticipation. She became all too aware of the warmth of his flesh, of his hand massaging her back through her cotton sweater. His scent was stimulating, and she couldn't avoid breathing deeply of him.

The composure she'd managed to maintain was quickly crumbling. Though his eyes glittered with resentment, she had the oddest sensation that mingled with all that passionate dislike there was a flicker of attraction, that his gaze was echoing the erotic lyrics of the song. "Shut up and kiss me!" "Shut up and kiss me!" "Shut up and kiss me, *Amy...*"

She stumbled, going faint at the very idea. *Could he possibly be saying he wanted to kiss her? And horror of horrors—did she have the remotest desire to kiss him back?*

Noting her unsteadiness, he gathered her more securely against him. "Maybe I should have a few beers," he said softly. "I'd be more what you're used to."

She found herself shyly smiling and wondering at herself. Before she could make any sense of the see-sawing of her emotions, the song ended and a drumroll sounded.

There was a fraction of a second hesitation before Beau released her so that she could face the platform. When she was set free, she separated herself to a safer distance and focused her attention on Mr. Jones, their host. He stood before the five-piece band and beamed down at his guests. A wiry man with a strong, angular face, Al Jones was dressed in jeans, brown roper boots and a green-and-yellow plaid shirt. He sported a thick shock of silver hair, keen black eyes, a blade-sharp nose and affectionate smile that reminded her of Ira. Her mood darkened, and she had no idea why.

"Folks," Al began, raising his hands for silence, "I don't mean to spoil the fun with a lot of jabberin', but I figure since it's my barn, I can speak my mind." He wagged thick gray brows and grinned as his guests chortled. He lifted his hands for quiet. "It's time I said my piece about why Edna and I invited you all over here on this cold Valentine's Day."

Amy experienced a stab at the reminder of what day it was, and that she was supposed to have been married today.

"Come on up here, sugar." Al gestured for his wife to join him. In her starched jeans, fancy boots and red ruffled shirt, Edna clambered up the wobbly bales. She was a spry, narrow-waisted, wide-hipped woman with rosy cheeks and a cap of curly gray hair. Though she wasn't classically pretty, her sweetness shone so brightly in her button-brown eyes, she seemed striking. What a dear couple they made. And they seemed so in love.

Al put an arm around his wife's waist and cleared his throat. "Edna and I are glad to be sharing our happiness with all our friends this evening. Getting to share fifty choice years with this woman is celebration enough for me, but, heck, a party's nice any time." He bent to kiss Edna's temple. "I'm the luckiest man on this crazy ol' earth, and I only hope every one of you sons of bucks in my barn here finds the same brand of love in your own lives. Makes this hard, back-country life worth the livin'."

Edna gave him a loving pat on the cheek, her face going an attractive crimson as she accepted his words of love. The two kissed amid sighs from the onlooking women and laughter and applause from the men. The couple became a blurry picture to Amy, and she discovered she was crying. Al Jones's statement had been far from flowery and as simple a declaration of devotion as she'd ever heard, yet it touched her deeply. Even frightened her, somehow. This sweet couple seemed to have found that elusive thing called love. It was obvious, glimmering in their eyes, even after all these years.

She hugged herself, unsettled by the discovery. Could she be making a mistake by marrying Ira? Could there be someone out there she should wait for—her true love?

She tried to shake off the thought. Ira was a wonderful, kind man. After all, Amy's mother, Louise, had married a man she hardly knew. Louise's parents had arranged for her to marry a man much older than she was. Amy remembered her mother telling her that when Amy's grandfather had suffered a bad heart attack, he'd decided to find a stable home for his only daughter, Louise, and had chosen to marry her off to a family friend, Bill Vale. A high school teacher in Chicago, Bill Vale was twenty years Louise's senior.

Amy's mother had said her relationship with Bill had been platonic for nearly two years after their marriage, and that Amy's father had been a patient, compassionate man. Only after Louise had grown extremely fond of him had their marriage grown intimate.

Louise and Bill Vale had been a contented couple all Amy's life. She'd never heard her mother mention being head-over-heels in love with her father. Louise Vale had used words like "comfortable", and "compatible", and had seemed satisfied with her life. Until this minute, Amy had thought consideration and shared interests were what counted, not some intangible entity called "love".

She gave Al and Edna Jones another glance. They were arm in arm as Al helped his wife down from the platform. He kissed her lightly on the cheek, and they exchanged smiles as the band struck up a waltz. Couples came together and began to slow dance.

Unsettled, Amy sidled away, not daring to look at Beau. A thought nagged, upsetting her further. Could he possibly be right about her? Was she marrying Ira for his money? Would she have rushed into accepting his proposal if it hadn't been for Mary's situation and his offer to help?

No! she told herself. She *wasn't* a money-grubbing bimbo. She truly wanted to make a good life on Diablo Butte, to be Ira's wife—the best rancher's wife in Wyoming.

Feeling queasy, she swallowed several times. The welcome warmth of the barn had become stifling. Maybe she needed fresh air. Yes, that was it. All she needed was a little fresh air and she'd be fine.

Hurrying out the side door, she took in a knife-sharp breath and headed away from the barn. The snow crunched beneath her feet as she broke through the frozen crust, her skirt flirting with the surface as she dashed away.

She reached a pine tree, its lower branches cut away, and leaned against the trunk, huffing and puffing. Squeezing her eyes closed, she attempted to shut everything from her mind. She *was* doing the right thing, marrying Ira. Maybe Al and Edna had been matched up by their own parents fifty years ago. Lots of people came together in arranged marriages all over the world, and many worked out fine, didn't they? Most of them weren't in love in the beginning, were they?

Her teeth chattered as the cold began to penetrate. Pressing her hands to her cheeks, she was surprised to discover how hot they were. With a sigh, she sagged farther against the rough tree trunk, hardly registering that her body was raked by shivers.

"Are you nuts?"

She jerked around to see Beau stalking toward her. "Have you ever heard of hypothermia?"

She wasn't in the mood for his browbeating. "I d-don't know. Hum a few bars and maybe it'll c-come to me."

He shrugged out of his coat, putting it around her quaking shoulders. "From what I hear, suddenly gaining a sense of humor is one of the danger signs that you're freezing to death."

She sniffed disdainfully. "Well, *you're* obviously in n-no danger." His coat felt like sunlight itself, for it held the radiant warmth of his body.

"What are you doing out here?"

She deliberately faced away from him, restively tracing along the scabrous trunk in pretended nonchalance. "I wanted to think."

"Something wrong?"

He sounded almost interested, but it might be a trick of the cold on her frozen eardrums. She shook her head. "Go back inside. You'll get cold."

"Do you want to go home?"

Surprised by the question, she shifted to face him. "Wouldn't that spoil your fun? I mean, leaving all your devoted lady friends behind?"

He shrugged his hands into his jeans pockets and nearly smiled. "I'd be devastated."

His tone told her he didn't care one way or the other. "Then what about Cookie and Archie?"

"They have to get up early. They won't care."

"No." She toyed with her lower lip. "I'm fine. Really. I just needed some air."

"And to think," he added.

"Right." Her glance veered away. His dubious expression told her he knew something was wrong, but she had no intention of telling him what it was.

"Need more time to think?"

She didn't know if he was teasing her or not, but she decided to ignore it if he was. She was too emotionally spent to fight. "No, I'm all done." Avoiding eyes she feared might be glittering with wry amusement, she added, "Lucky I'm a fast thinker." Intent on going inside, she stepped away from the tree.

"I've been thinking, too."

Curious, she peered his way. She was afraid she'd regret it if she took the bait, but for some reason she couldn't help herself. "Thinking? All by yourself?" Now that she wasn't freezing anymore, she felt more sure of herself. Why not give him a taste of his own medicine?

He surprised her with one of his charming grins, and a tiny tingle raced through her at the sight. "Don't be bashful," he coaxed, lounging casually against the tree. "Tell me how you *really* feel." As he spoke, his breath clouded in the air. It was awfully cold, and even though he wore a heavy off-white sweater layered over a navy turtleneck, he had to be feeling it.

"Maybe we'd better go inside." She took a step in the direction of the barn.

He moved into her path. "Wouldn't you like to know what I've been thinking?"

His face was silhouetted against the soft moonlight, but even in the duskiness, his eyes riveted her to the spot. "Uh—actually, Mr. Diablo, I don't think I need to know—"

"I was thinking, since I won't be attending the wedding, maybe I'd better kiss the bride—now."

She blinked up at him, positive she'd misunderstood. But before she could ask him to repeat himself, his large hands were holding her face, his lips covering hers with a kiss that was disconcertingly tender. Amy realized for the first time that she'd imagined this man's kisses—hot, demanding, angry. But never gentle, never giving. This kiss was startlingly loving as his lips feather-touched hers in soft persuasion.

What was this? What did he think he was doing? If this was intended to be a chaste token between relatives, then he was sadly mistaken about the effect of his kisses. The tenderness of his lips sent sparks rushing through her veins, drugged her senses, and she found herself reaching up, clinging to him to keep from collapsing in a heap.

She heard herself moan as his mouth slanted across hers, caressing, lightly coaxing her lips apart. The subtle invitation was deliciously sensual and she responded by doing exactly what he'd slyly demanded, her lips parting joyfully.

He released her face and slipped his hands beneath the coat draped from her shoulders. Massaging her back, he moved his hands downward, delighting her flesh. She was stunned to find herself pressed wantonly against him, relishing his potent maleness, craving even more seductive stroking from his talented fingers. Her woman's intuition told her he would be a magnificent lover, and somewhere deep inside, a need awakened in her to know the full depth of his passion.

She felt luscious jolt after jolt as his tongue did wild, wonderful things to the sensitive recesses of her mouth. Some little voice in her brain was shrieking that this was scandalous. Wasn't this supposed to have been *her* wedding day? Didn't she plan to be Ira Diablo's wife? If so, then why was she kissing Beau Diablo so madly? *Why?*

The little voice was starting to penetrate through to her desire-numbed mind, and she grew mortified at what she'd allowed to happen. Her fingers were wound in the soft hair at Beau's nape, and she tried desperately to compel her hands to let go, push him away, but her limbs were simply not obeying.

Suddenly, he lifted his face from her throbbing lips, abruptly stepping away. Amy thought he staggered slightly, but she couldn't trust her own senses. Helpless, she slumped against the tree, holding on for dear life. Shamed, she hugged the trunk and leaned her fiery cheek against the cold, craggy bark.

"Dammit," Beau growled.

She tilted her face his way, breathing heavily. "You did that on purpose," she moaned, her words thick and sluggish.

He ran a hand through his hair without responding, but his jaw worked ferociously.

"That didn't prove I'm cheap!" she cried.

He gave her a malevolent look. "Who are you trying to convince, Miss Vale? Me—or you?"

"I've been kissed a few times, and you *meant* that one." She swallowed several times to clear the huskiness from her voice. "Don't tell me you didn't mean it!" She wasn't sure why she had to say that, but she did.

"What do you want from me? Sure, I meant it," he said, his voice hard. "I've already told you you're damn beautiful and I'd share a blanket with you any time. We'd be good in bed, and you know it."

Her heart stopped beating as he confirmed her worst fear. It would have been fine with him if he'd killed two birds with one stone—proved she had loose morals, and had an hour or so of meaningless sex in the process. It was all so cruelly calculated she wanted to scream. But something inside her was too broken apart for her to even stand without support. Closing her eyes, she turned away. "You don't think much of me, do you?"

"On the contrary," he said grimly, "I don't think of you at all."

When she looked at him again, her eyes were swimming with tears. "I've changed my mind. I'd like to go home." She was grateful the words came out as calmly as they did.

Nodding almost imperceptibly, he turned on his heel and headed toward the barn. She watched him go, watched his hard, powerful body, the same glorious body she'd so recently clutched and craved. Choking, she covered her mouth with her hands, fearing she would burst out sobbing if she didn't.

Before Beau entered the barn, he stopped and leaned a shoulder against the wall, apparently taking a restorative breath. He shocked her by turning her way, his expression grave as their eyes locked. Time seemed to slow, then stop as they stared across the shadowy stillness. Caught in the snare of his gaze, a painful irony engulfed her. Why had she never felt this connected to anyone else in her life—yet felt so completely alone?

CHAPTER SEVEN

WHEN Amy regained her senses, she realized she was being rude not to make her own goodbyes. She rushed inside and found Al and Edna Jones, then wished them fifty more happy years together. Then she shrugged out of Beau's coat and wordlessly handed it to him, tugging her own parka from his hand. She had no intention of allowing him to help her with it. She'd had enough fake gallantry for one evening.

Once they were loaded in the sleigh and bundled up, Beau headed away from the barn and out of the valley. Music resonated through the night for a long time after they left: happy, bright, spirited music, much like the rugged, hardworking people she'd met since coming to Wyoming. She'd become fond of the people very quickly, which only strengthened her original plans to make a good life for herself out here with Ira.

The only flaw in her plan was the fact that after her marriage she'd be related to Beau Diablo. The idea of seeing him, even on an occasional basis, was disturbing. His kiss had been a well-crafted act of sabotage. She didn't know why he'd bothered, since his relationship with his father wasn't close. Why should he care how many times his father got married? Maybe he just wanted to prove to himself that he was right, or demonstrate very graphically to her that she was no more honorable than Ira's other wives. So he'd used his subtle male expertise to catch her off guard and make her slip helplessly into his arms.

She glared in his direction as he lead the team along a moonlit trail that mocked her with its romantic beauty. Beau was very good at seduction. With every muscle, every fiber of her being, she wanted to leap up and shout that he had been ruthlessly unfair, kissing her the way he had. A few very select, very skillful men knew how to turn cold marble into molten lava with their kisses. That didn't mean the marble had been scheming to erupt into a fountain of sparks, ash and liquid rock, did it? So what if Beau Diablo was sexy. So what if he knew how to make a woman want him. That didn't mean she wasn't completely honest about her desire to make a good marriage to Ira.

She had an almost overpowering urge to scream, *"There should be a law against kissing like that! You should wear a warning label!"* She wondered how many poor, unsuspecting women had been led astray by those clever lips. Well, she didn't intend to be one of them. Her life's plan was made. She wouldn't be put on the defensive by his cold-blooded ploy; she wouldn't be made to feel guilty or wrong, darn him!

"Say, Amy, hon?" Cookie piped up, drawing her from her mental struggles.

"Yes?" Silently, she blessed the housekeeper for speaking. Any subject would be better than dwelling on Beau's kisses.

"You never said where your folks are. Do they live in Chicago, too?"

Sadness pricked her heart. "My parents passed away." She shifted to face Archie and Cookie, careful not to brush against Beau as she did. Their expressions were clear in the moonglow and she watched their smiles fade with her news. "A plane crash five years ago," she explained somberly. "I'd just graduated from high school and had been accepted at Northwestern on a scholarship. We were taking a trip to Florida as a combination celebration-vacation." She cleared her throat, surprised that after all these years it was still hard to talk about. "I was lucky. I just broke a leg. My sister—" She cut herself off. She hadn't meant to say anything about Mary.

"Oh, Lordy!" Cookie clutched her gloved hands to her breasts. "Please don't tell me you lost a sister in the crash, too."

Realizing it was too late to take back the admission, she shook her head, peeking at Beau. He was staring ahead, apparently disinterested in her chatter. "Mary's my sister's name. She was hurt badly, but the doctors think this last operation might finally help her walk again."

"How old is she?" Archie asked, his beefy face troubled.

"Sixteen." Amy smiled, thinking of her sister. "She's a great kid. Never complains. I know she'll walk again."

"Must be pretty expensive, those operations," Cookie said. "What about your schooling?"

Amy dropped her gaze to the hand she had draped along the back of the seat. She was clinching it into a fist and forced herself to relax, though the subject was difficult to deal with. "Well, naturally, I couldn't afford to go to college after my folks—died. But their insurance helped pay for Mary's operations. At least up until this last one. It's pretty much gone now."

"You poor kid." Cookie shook her head, tugging her wool cap more tightly over her ears. "You've been supporting yourself and your little sis all this time—by yourself?"

Amy's cheeks flamed with embarrassment. She'd never gotten used to the sound of pity in people's voices, no matter how well-meaning they were. "I found a job with pretty good tips." She shrugged it off. "We've done okay."

"Where's your sister now?" Archie asked.

"A convalescent home in Chicago. As soon as she's better, Ira said she can join us."

"That's dandy." Cookie's smile returned. "I always said, there's nothin' like fresh air to heal a person. She'll cure up fine once she gets out of that big, dirty town."

Amy had to grin at Cookie's description of Chicago. Obviously, she didn't think much of city life. "I hope you're right."

"The operation was a success?" Archie asked.

"The doctors thought the prognosis was good when I left."

"Miss Vale," Beau interrupted brusquely, "don't you care how your sister is doing now?"

She veered his way, breathing fire. "How dare you ask me such a question?"

"Then why haven't you called her?"

Furious that he would suggest that she didn't care about Mary, she had difficulty keeping her rage under control. "Since I'm *obviously* a burden to you, I didn't want to trespass on your hospitality any more than I already have."

His jaw tightened. "Call your sister, dammit. Why would you think you couldn't?"

She heaved a groan. "You have the most irritating talent for making me feel wrong when I'm not!"

The stillness became oppressive, and Amy was mortified she'd let Cookie and Archie see the antagonism that simmered between her and their employer. She turned away, depressed. This Valentine's Day would go into her diary as one of her very worst— dead opposite from anything she'd imagined.

Hunching down in her blanket, she tried to absorb every ounce of warmth it had to offer. Though she would never admit it, she was uncomfortably cold. She didn't think she was freezing to death, for she'd read somewhere that freezing people started to feel nice and warm and drowsy. She was neither warm nor sleepy. She was cold and mad. Unfortunately, she was also quivering like a striptease dancer.

"Slide over, Miss Vale."

She glanced his way, then slid to the edge of the sleigh. "Far enough?"

"I meant toward me," he corrected, impatience in his tone. "Slip the blanket over my legs so my body heat can warm you."

She was so hostile to the idea, she found herself hesitating even as another bone-jarring tremor shook her body. "I—I find the brisk air invigorating."

"If you like shaking, you'll love pneumonia." He grasped her wrist, drawing her close. "I told my father I'd keep you from freezing to death. I keep my promises."

The next thing she knew, she was snuggled hip to thigh against him, aggravated that their close proximity was so foolishly welcome in some primal, womanly part of her—the same foolish womanly place that refused to let her forget his kiss.

The stillness was punctuated only by jingling bells and the mingled snores of the couple in the back of the sleigh, who apparently were able to drop off to sleep at the speed of light. Amy would have preferred that they remained awake and all joined in singing one hundred rousing choruses of "Ninety-nine Bottles of Beer on the Wall". She hated the grinding repetitiveness of the ditty and had heard it in the cowboy bar more times than she cared to recall. But this forced confinement beneath a shared blanket, wrapped in Beau's warmth, brought unfamiliar senses to life inside her that were as disturbing as the touch of his lips.

His arm slid around her shoulders, hugging her against him, and she jumped in surprise.

"Getting warmer?" he queried softly, so as not to awaken their sleeping passengers.

His chest was solid and inviting, his scent hypnotic. If she were to tell him the whole, ugly truth, she'd have to say she was sizzling, but she had a feeling he was referring to the environment, not her libido. "Yes—thank you," she mumbled, deciding there was no point in arguing. It would serve no purpose except to wake Archie and Cookie. She might as well accept his warmth humbly and remember to keep her distance from now on.

"Sleepy?"

"No."

"Go ahead and sleep, if you want. It'll be another half hour before we get home."

"I don't think so," she grumbled. Why did the Wyoming winter night have to be so wildly beautiful and the sleigh ride such an idyllic setting, with bells jangling and sturdy horses prancing through snow luminescent in the moonlight? Why did a bizarre feeling of having come home niggle at her brain?

"A nap would do you good." The statement came quietly, hardly discernible over the tinkling of the bells. "If you're worried, I don't attack unconscious women."

She shot him a sharp look and was sorry she did. His eyes glowed strangely in the dimness, and her throat constricted. After several ponderous seconds, she found her voice, rasping, "*Now* you tell me the rules!"

His lips quirked. "If you'd rather drive the sleigh, I'll sleep."

"Fine!" she retorted. "I just hope these horses are half bloodhound or we might end up in Japan."

He handed her the reins. "Good night, Miss Vale."

She stared, incredulous. "You can't mean it!"

"Hush. I'm trying to sleep." He leaned back, tugging his Stetson brim down over his eyes.

She held the reins warily, muttering under her breath, "I *hate* you."

He smiled, but otherwise didn't move. "I gave you your chance to sleep."

"I hope we *do* end up in Japan. I assume these horses are good swimmers, because sooner or later—"

"Just one question," he interrupted, prodding his hat brim up with a thumb and eyeing her speculatively. "Do *you* attack unconscious men?"

She stared openmouthed. How dare he goad her so unmercifully? The egotistical bum! She thrust the reins into his lap. "You know—the idea *is* appealing. It's just a shame I forgot my ax!"

His low chuckle warmed the chilly night.

*   *   *

Amy awoke at dawn to bad news. Snow was spinning and swirling outside her window. It wasn't a blizzard, but it was coming down hard enough to spell the end to her hopes of getting to Diablo Butte today.

Pushing up to sit, she brushed her hair back, dejection flooding through her. She shook her head in a physical effort to throw off her depression. "Getting upset about it won't help, Amy. Work will take your mind off—everything. So get up and get busy."

Ten minutes later, she was hanging her parka on a peg in the cook house, ready to help Archie and Cookie make breakfast. For a change, Archie was nowhere to be found and Cookie was measuring out flour for biscuits.

Amy plucked a dish towel from a drawer and tied a makeshift apron around her middle. "What do I do?" she asked. "I'm getting pretty good at coffee and bacon. Maybe I ought to start there." She grinned at the older woman and headed to the nearest industrial-size refrigerator without waiting for a reply.

"Sounds good, hon," Cookie called over her shoulder as she worked at the room's center island work space. "We're startin' to make a pretty fair team."

Amy laughed and grabbed the plastic container of thick-sliced bacon. "Sure. You and Archie do the cooking and I do the burning."

Cookie chortled. "Now, that was jes' that one batch of biscuits. You're doing better'n Archie does most days, truth told."

Amy started bacon frying, then measured out the coffee. "Speaking of Archie..." She came over to Cookie's side. "Is he sleeping in this morning?"

Cookie grimaced and shook her head. "Bursitis has got him movin' slow, poor darlin'."

That reminded Amy of something. "By the way, how many years have you and Archie been married? Did you ever figure it out?"

Cookie smirked. "Been married thirty-three years, but I got the old fool convinced it's thirty-five. So, next week about now, he's givin' me one of them relax-o-lounge chairs. You know, the kind that sits up or lays back."

Amy nodded, having seen the commercials on TV. "So the thirty-fifth anniversary is the 'relax-o-lounge' anniversary?"

Cookie guffawed as she stirred the biscuit makings. "Heck if I know. But that's what I want, so that's what I told him."

Amy had begun cracking eggs into a bowl but stopped to grin at her companion. "What a sneak you are."

Cookie winked. "Hon, when you've been married as long as me, you'll know these men don't know a thing about shoppin', so you give 'em any good reason not to and they won't *have* to shop. They just buy what you say."

Amy lifted her brows, nodding sagely. "Sounds like a good plan."

The two woman were silent for a few minutes while Cookie got her first batch of biscuits into the oven. Amy dumped the eggs and other ingredients into a frying pan and was dutifully tending both eggs and bacon when she was startled to find Cookie lurking at her elbow. She turned, curious. "Anything wrong?" The housekeeper's normally jolly expression had gone somber. "Have I done something wrong?"

The housekeeper put a companionable hand on Amy's shoulder. "Not a drop, hon." She paused, appearing to vacillate about something. After a minute, she patted Amy's shoulder again, her decision made. "It's just that I figured you should know something, seeing how you're gettin' ready to marry into the Diablo family."

Amy grew apprehensive and fumbled with her cooking fork. "What is it?" she asked, not sure she wanted to know.

Cookie heaved a deep breath and removed her hand from Amy's shoulder to absently wipe it on her apron. "Well, it's like this." Her brows knit contemplatively. "I saw the way you and Mr. Beau was outa sorts with each other last night, and I figure it's because of what his daddy done these last years. You may already know, but they ain't real close."

Amy nodded. "I gathered that."

Cookie shrugged. "Now, I ain't speaking bad of Mr. Ira. Every man's gotta live his own life. It's jes' that when he divorced Beau's ma, Mrs. Pamela, nine years ago, it tore her up pretty bad. Mrs. Pamela and Mr. Ira been married near thirty years. Poor Mrs. Pamela came to stay with her boy. Mr. Beau had to watch his mama waste away and die. She lived long enough to see her Ira cavort with one trashy woman after another, then marry that first one. That blow to her heart finished her, I figure." She plucked a checkered handkerchief from her hip pocket and noisily wiped at her nose. "Mr. Beau ain't never forgave his daddy for tossin' his mama off that cold way."

Cookie screwed up her face, clearly not wanting to say something else, but deciding she must. "This is nothin' against you, Miss Amy. You're a lady. I saw that the first day you worried 'bout me carryin' your bag for you. But Beau's heart was beat down when his mama died, and I don't figure he's seeing Ira's newest fiancée with such a clear eye as me. All them other women of Ira's was nothin' but a bunch of low-down trash."

As Cookie stuffed the handkerchief away, Amy winced. Maybe it *had* been kinder of Beau not to introduce her as Ira's fiancée, if this was the reputation his previous wives had around here.

"No offense, hon. But that's the way it is." She took the cooking fork from Amy's slack hand. It was the first time she noticed she'd gone still. How sad for Beau to have had to helplessly watch his mother die from grieving over her lost love. No wonder he didn't care much for his father or his string of young wives.

Cookie absently poked at the bacon. "So, if Mr. Beau acts like he's lookin' for a hog to kick, I was hoping you'd give him a little rope. He's a fair man. But if I say so myself, his papa's foolin' around made him miserable as a cowpoke ridin' night herd in freezing rain." With an encouraging grin, she added, "Jes' keep being the nice person I see, and one of these days he'll accept how different you are from them other gals. I swear he will."

There was a banging sound behind them, indicating the first of the hungry cowboys were gathering to eat. Amy's throat had closed, and she couldn't speak around the lump that had formed there. After what Cookie had said, she could hardly blame Beau

for having a chip on his shoulder. Nodding mutely at
the housekeeper, she took back the fork. "Thanks for
telling me," she managed. As the older woman started
to move away, Amy took her hand. "And, Cookie,
I—I really believe Ira's seen his mistake. It'll work
this time."

The housekeeper's eyes glimmered with compassion. Turning Amy's hand into her own callused
one, she squeezed. "You're a fine person, hon. And
for your sake, I'll pray it's true."

"*Coffee!*" bellowed one of the wranglers.

"You better have two broke feet, Willie Stumpet,
shoutin' at me thata way," Cookie bellowed back.
"Maybe you just got one good eye, but I figure you
can see we're shorthanded here."

The weathered cowhand hee-hawed and ambled to
the shelf where the coffee mugs were housed. "Miss
Amy." He greeted her with a nod. "Don't let that
bossy old stretch o' barbed wire teach you to be crusty
and mean. You stay sweet and pretty like you are."

Amy felt a blush rush up her face, but before she
could respond, Cookie retorted, "I'd watch the name-
callin', you old slab of buzzard bait, or you'll be sorry
the next time you want your grubby clothes washed."

Good-natured banter filled the room as more and
more cowhands blew in with the frolicking snow. Amy
busied herself filling plates. But as busy as she got,
she couldn't stop thinking about Beau's mother and
about Ira's treatment of her.

Though outwardly happy, she was far from it. Inwardly, she was eaten up with anxiety. Ira had admitted he'd done some stupid things in his past. He'd
assured her he'd changed and learned the hard way

what was important in life.

Surely that was true.

The day had been long and cold for everyone. Amy was tired and hungry, but she stopped by the pen that held the new calves to visit with Desiree. Her little chats with the calf had become the most enjoyable part of her day.

Once in the cook house, Archie had dinner ready, and when Amy began to help serve, he shooed her away. "No, you don't, Miss Amy. You work with them hands all day. I ain't lettin' you come back here and work in the kitchen, too. Have yourself a cup of coffee and relax there by the fire like the rest of them wranglers."

Amy was too tired to argue. As she poured herself some of the strong stuff, she had to admit she could hardly lift the mug, let alone do much cooking. "Something smells good," she said, taking a sip.

"That's a world-famous recipe of mine cookin'."

Amy nodded. "Smells like it must be famous."

"Won first place ten years runnin' at the State Fair," Archie boasted, lifting the lid on a skillet to scan the contents. "Now, you go sit yourself down. Supper's near done."

She took a seat on the bench. Mysteriously, there'd been a spot left vacant in front of the fire. She knew that to be the most coveted location after a long, cold workday, and she had a feeling the men were being gallant, leaving it for her. Silently, she blessed every scraggly whisker on their faces. She was bone chilled, and the heat of that blaze meant more to her than a million-dollar diamond ever could.

The cowhands kept her laughing with hilarious ranching stories as their supper was served. Beau joined them late, taking a seat across from Amy just as she had her first taste of what she assumed to be chicken nuggets. It didn't taste quite like chicken nuggets, however. Trying to avoid eye contact with her host, she turned toward Snapper, sitting on her right. "This doesn't taste like chicken, but it's good. What is it?"

Snapper had taken a mouthful of mashed potatoes, and tried spasmodically to swallow so he could respond.

"Mountain oysters," Beau said before Snapper could speak.

Her gaze drifted to his face with reluctance. "Mountain oysters?" she repeated, not sure she'd heard right. "I've never heard of them."

Beau's lips twitched and Amy noticed the other cowhands had stopped eating. She looked around, wondering why they were all so intent on her comment about the dinner. "Do you like them?" he asked.

Amy didn't trust the twinkle in his eyes. "They're fine." She started to worry. "Why do I have a feeling they're not oysters at all?"

A couple of the cowboys snickered and a tremor went up her spine.

Suddenly feeling a little sick, she placed her fork on her plate and stared at Beau. "It's something disgusting, isn't it—like rattlesnake patties or possum tongues?"

"We learned long ago not to waste anything out here, Miss Vale," Beau said, taking a bite.

She pulled her lips between her teeth, fairly sure she was turning green. "Oh, no—it's worse than I thought."

After finishing the mouthful, he went on, "Every spring when we castrate the calves, we toss the testicles in a bucket and—"

Amy's jaw dropped. "Oh—my—heaven!" She moaned, launching herself from the bench. "Oh—dear . . ." Nauseous, she lurched away from the table and grabbed her parka. She dashed out into the snow, hoping the slap of cold air would keep her from being sick.

She was leaning against the log wall, her eyes closed and inhaling deeply, when she heard the door open and close. Someone had come outside. She hoped it was Cookie checking on her, but she didn't dare open her eyes to be sure. Instead she just inhaled again, fighting nausea.

"The best rancher's wife in Wyoming wouldn't be your shade of green."

Her stomach reeled, but she held herself under control. "You enjoyed that, didn't you?" she mumbled between clenched teeth.

"Miss Vale," he said, sounding very close, "it's a prank we play on city people. If it makes you feel any better, most folks new to ranching areas react the way you did."

She opened one eye, feeling a little less like dying. "You people need to find some hobbies."

He grinned, lounging against the wall. "Don't tell me you wouldn't get a chuckle out of watching some hayseed trying to figure out how to eat his first lobster?"

She opened her other eye and lifted her chin. "It's not the same thing at all."

"How so?"

She wasn't sure her argument was on solid ground, but she refused to admit it. "Because—because a lobster is not an obscene part of a *cow*, that's how so!"

He chuckled. "I can't argue that."

She found herself smiling back and realized she didn't feel sick any longer. As a matter of fact, she felt a bit *too* good. It amazed her how quickly Beau's charisma could affect her. She didn't like that about herself, and she quickly sobered. "I—I hope I didn't hurt Archie's feelings."

"He'll live."

She eyed heaven, wanting to do the brave thing— go back in there and eat Archie's prizewinning mountain oysters, but she was highly doubtful that she could.

"Did you call your sister today?" he asked, startling her with the change of subject.

Wanting to avoid the troubles that came with looking at his handsome face, she stared past him. Snow danced through a shaft of golden light from one of the cook-house windows. "I—I thought I should wait until the rates went down in the evening."

"Go call her, Miss Vale," he commanded quietly. "Now."

She shifted her unwilling gaze to meet his. Several snowflakes had settled on his long black eyelashes. Melting with his body warmth, they sparkled like precious gems. Her heart skipped two consecutive beats at the sight, and the memory of his kiss came flooding back. Hurriedly, she moved away from his disconcerting nearness. "I think I will," she whispered, making a brisk escape toward the ranch house.

"By the way..."

She didn't want to stop, didn't want to turn back, but she forced herself, though she kept her glance focused no higher than his feet. "Yes?"

"Ira's been trying to call you on his shortwave radio." He continued to lounge against the wall, lifting one boot to rest against the wood. "Apparently our radio's been broken. I fixed it today."

Amy frowned, skeptical at the nonchalant tone. Why did she have the sneaking suspicion he'd purposely pulled out a wire or loosened a tube to keep her from talking to his father? What could he hope to gain, except maybe an opportunity to work her so hard she'd run screaming back to Chicago before Ira could talk her out of it? It would be just like Beau Diablo to pull such a dirty trick. "How did you discover it was broken?" she asked, the tightness in her voice revealing her distrust.

He shrugged, and it was the first time she became aware that she'd lifted her gaze. "Al Jones told me last night that Ira radioed him and asked if we were all dead out here."

A stinging accusation was on the tip of her tongue, and she wanted to shout, *"Lucky there was a party or your trickery would never have been found out!"* She didn't know if it was prudence or cowardice, but she decided not to blurt her indictment. Instead she began to back away. "Lucky there was a party, then."

"Lucky," he agreed with a shrug.

Her anger building, she halted, eyeing him narrowly. "So, how do I use this radio?"

"If you'd like, after dinner I'll radio Ira for you. You can speak to him then."

"If I'd *like*?" she echoed, incredulous. Spinning away, she tromped off. "Don't go to any trouble on *my* account, Mr. Diablo!"

"No trouble at all, Miss Vale," he assured her with infuriating politeness.

CHAPTER EIGHT

AMY had never been in the bunkhouse before, so she hadn't been aware Beau owned a shortwave radio. He'd sent her a message through Cookie to meet him there, and he would radio Ira for her. When she arrived, she entered to find a long, barrackslike room similar to the cook house, but without cooking facilities.

At the end where she entered, there were several easy chairs scattered around next to table lamps or standing lamps. A couple of wranglers looked up from books and smiled. J.C., the man with the cracked ribs, grinned at her through his chest-length beard, and continued to puff on a pipe that gave off a mellow cherry scent. She smiled back. "Mr. Diablo sent for me."

J.C. nodded his balding head. "Probably be right here, miss," he said, his teeth clenched around his pipe. She wanted to ask him how his ribs were, but decided he'd be embarrassed. Nodding, she turned away and scanned a bookcase, filled with dog-eared novels, that dominated the front wall. Colorful woven rugs dotted the plank floor giving the room its only touches of color—except for the colorfully clad cowhands.

In one corner sat a card table. Four folding chairs stood away from the table as though they'd been left in haste—probably about the time the blizzard hit—and hadn't been used since.

131

Midway into the sparsely furnished room, there were six sets of bunk beds, three to a side, all neatly made. A couple of off-duty hands were dozing, oblivious to lights or conversation. Wooden lockers were fastened to the wall between the beds. The rear of the long room held a couple of doors. Amy assumed they led to the bath and shower.

There was no fireplace in the bunkhouse, but there were a couple of butane stoves, one in front and one in back. Even so, the room was a little cool for her tastes. She decided not to take off her parka or she'd have to huddle by one of the stoves. Besides, she wouldn't be here long. Since the shortwave radio was sitting right next to the card table, she had a feeling there would be absolutely no privacy, so the conversation would be short and discreet.

The door burst open, and Amy thought it was Beau, but instead she saw Snapper dash in, his face even more red than usual. "Come on, J.C." He darted to the bunks and swatted at the sleeping men to rouse them. "Marv! Ed! We got a cow down in the north pasture and the boss said to get her on the downer cow skid as quick as possible."

J.C. and the others were up and pulling on coats and gloves almost before Snapper's words were out. "Can I help?" she asked.

Snapper grinned shyly. "No, ma'am. We got it handled."

"What's wrong with the cow?"

"Slipped on ice. She'll be okay once we get her to solid ground. But right now she can't get her footin'."

"Poor thing," Amy mused as the men filed out into the cold night.

After the noise of tromping boots and the slamming door, the place seemed eerily quiet. She could hear the hiss of the nearby butane stove and the tick of a clock she hadn't yet spotted. Looking around, she spied it: a little cuckoo with painted alps and a mountain chalet above the clock face was nailed to the wall above one of the lower bunks. Its hands showed the time as a few minutes after seven. She'd just missed the birdie, or chalet owner, or whatever it might be, make his seven o'clock appearance.

The door squeaked again, and she stiffened. The authoritative tread on the floor had a disturbingly familiar sound. "Sorry to keep you waiting," he said, not sounding sorry at all.

She turned, her expression as stiff as her posture. "I just got here," she lied. For all she knew he'd been lurking outside and knew exactly how long he'd kept her cooling her heels. "Will that cow be okay?"

He'd slid out of his jacket and was hanging it on a peg. He frowned her way. "What cow?"

"The one that slipped on the ice."

He deposited his Stetson on a second hook. "It'll be fine, since Willie spotted it. If it'd been down all night, it could have frozen to death."

She bit her lip. "You deal with a lot of life and death things out here."

He scanned her face, his expression cool. "Nature can be cruel, Miss Vale."

She nodded. "Still, it must be hard some days...."

"Getting cold feet?" He headed toward the corner where the shortwave was housed.

"My feet have been cold for days, Mr. Diablo. But if you mean, am I changing my mind, the answer's no." She joined him as he sat down before the radio, and for some reason found herself tugging her coat more closely around her. His attitude was decidedly chilly this evening. Adding ice to her tone so it would match his, she asked, "Could we get on with the call?"

He leaned back and grabbed the nearest folding chair and drew it up beside him. "Here, sit down."

She didn't like the idea, but had no intention of letting him think he frightened her. She plopped into the chair and listened in stoic silence while he radioed Diablo Butte. It took several attempts before someone came on the transceiver at the other end. The voice was full of static and definitely not Ira's. After telling the employee to get his father, Beau handed Amy the microphone. "Press this talk switch when you're speaking. When you're finished, let go. Got it?"

She nodded, hoping she did, but she hid her insecurity. "No problem."

He stood, but instead of leaving, he lingered. Amy couldn't see his expression without turning and she didn't want him to know she was even aware that he hadn't disappeared in a puff of black smoke. But she was very aware of him, his scent taunted, his eyes burned into her. She shifted, crossed and uncrossed her legs, cleared her throat. Nothing worked to remove him from her consciousness.

"Did you talk to your sister?"

His curt question made her fumble with the mike in her hand. Getting hold of herself, she nodded. "She's doing fine." Unable to help it, she faced him and found herself smiling. It had been a real balm to her soul to have a nice visit with Mary.

He watched her, eyes brooding. "Call her tomorrow if you want." He pivoted away, apparently to give her privacy.

"Thank you," she murmured, truly meaning it. Though his brusque attitude dimmed her smile, she was more grateful for his permission to call Mary than she'd been for his food and shelter. She was sorry he disliked her so much that he couldn't accept her thanks with any friendliness.

He looked over his shoulder, clearly startled by her show of gratitude. He frowned, but before he could say anything, there was a squawk on the radio. Amy jumped as the jarring noise became Ira's voice. She turned toward the radio, straining to hear. "Is that you, little sweetheart?" came the cheery voice, sounding metallic.

Amy pressed the talk switch. "Hi, Ira. How are you?" She stopped, then belatedly remembered Beau's instructions and let go of the talk switch.

"I'm *lonely*, little one! But I bet you're having the worst of it, stuck there with my grouchy son." He laughed one of his melodious laughs she remembered so well, but she was surprised his joviality didn't lift her spirits. Far from it. She felt oddly distanced from him. Trying to shake off the feeling, sure it was prewedding jitters, she laughed back. "It's been an experience," she called into the microphone. "I've learned how to feed cattle and break up ice."

"The hell you say," Ira shouted back. "Well, don't worry about it, little one. Right after the wedding, I'm going to reward your patience about this damnable snow with a shopping spree in Paris. How does that sound?"

Amy was taken aback. "Oh—Ira. You never mentioned a honeymoon trip."

He laughed his big, happy laugh again. "Well, little one, to be honest, I can't leave the ranch right now. But I figured you'd want to get out of all this snow. And what's nicer than spending money in an exotic place to take your mind off lousy weather? You can stay until spring."

She stared at the microphone, far from thrilled with this news. Her plan had been to get to know her husband, learn about his ranch, become a real rancher's wife. Besides, she didn't want to be gone when Mary was ready to travel. "Ira—that's kind of you..." She stopped, grimacing. She didn't want to hurt his feelings, but she had to find a way to explain that she had no intention of chasing off to Europe.

"Sweetheart," he came back, and Amy realized she must have let go of the talk switch. "Cook's yelling at me to come to dinner or he'll toss it to the dogs. I'll talk to you tomorrow."

"Oh—okay..." She wanted more time to discuss this Paris trip with him, but was frustrated by the unnatural way she was having to do it. "Uh—goodbye, Ira."

There was nothing but static to answer her.

"Finished?"

She spun around. Beau was lounging against the far wall, certainly not far enough away to be out of earshot. She glared at him. "You should know if I'm finished or not. You could hear everything as well as I could."

He pushed away from the wall. "Sounds like these few days with a grouch are going to pay off royally."

His tone was so sarcastic, Amy found Cookie's request to give him a little rope an impossibility. How dare he eavesdrop and then make fun of her in the bargain. "Why, yes, it looks like it *is* going to pay off! I *adore* Paris. Enough to put up with the biggest grouch west of the Mississippi for an entire week!" Hopping up from the chair, she sailed past him, highly insulted. Most of what she blurted was a lie. But there was one part of her speech she meant. He *was* a grouch. Even his handsome face and sculptured body couldn't change that. "Good night, Mr. Diablo." She threw open the door and headed out into fluttering snow.

"*Au revoir, mademoiselle*," he drawled, cold irony in his voice.

Amy didn't know if she was more irritated or more hungry. If pressed for the truth, she was fairly sure she knew what was bothering her, but she preferred to think she was tossing and turning because she hadn't eaten dinner. The other possibility was too unsettling to dwell on.

Tossing off the covers, she got out of bed and dressed. She couldn't bear lying there with nothing to do but think! Grabbing her parka, she tiptoed through the house and into the kitchen, where she threw together a cheese sandwich, then slipped out the kitchen door. Another inch of snow had fallen since she'd gone to bed several hours ago. She decided that trudging to the barn in this bitter cold was exactly what she needed to work off her pent-up energy.

She ate the sandwich as she walked, downing the last bite when she reached the pen where Desiree was housed. Climbing through the rails, she softly called her little friend. After a minute, she saw the spindly baby amble over and bawl with recognition. Perching on the bottom fence rail, she hugged the calf. It was nice to be offered a tidbit of unqualified love, even if it was from a dumb animal that probably couldn't tell her from any of the other humans on the place. But she didn't care. She just needed some comfort and warmth. "How are you doing, Desiree?" She rubbed the calf's neck affectionately. "If you've got some time, I need to talk—woman to woman."

Right on cue, the baby bawled again, and Amy smiled. "Thanks, sweetie. I'll do the same for you, any time."

For several minutes, she stroked Desiree's silky back. She wasn't hungry any longer, but she didn't feel better. She'd been afraid all along that it hadn't been hunger keeping her awake. She opened her mouth, but couldn't voice her apprehensions. She wasn't sure if it was because her thoughts were too muddled to put into words, or if they were too horrible to say out loud.

Restive and anxious, she stroked the calf. The conversation with Ira last evening had struck fear in her heart. Was he really interested in a true wife, a true home? What if she was just another girl-toy to him? She hugged Desiree's neck, suddenly frightened.

She couldn't stand the idea of such a sham of a life. What should she do? Should she pack up and go back to Chicago? Or was she overreacting? Maybe all she had to do was have a nice, private talk with Ira, convince him she didn't need trips to Paris to make her happy. All she wanted was a stable, secure home and family, like the one her parents had made together.

"Okay, Desiree. Since I don't seem to be able to talk about it out loud, how are you at mental telepathy?" The calf blinked and she smiled wanly. "That good? Wonderful." She pressed her cheek against the calf's neck, pondering what she should do. She supposed she shouldn't act rashly. Maybe Ira was overcompensating out of his concern for her happiness. If she explained how she felt, everything would probably be fine, wouldn't it?

A tear slid down her cheek and she had to stifle a sob. "Oh—Desiree." She shook her head to staunch the afflicted words from flowing out. Still, her mind cried, *"Why do I have the feeling it's not that easy?"*

The calf wiped a sloppy tongue across her chin, seeming to show compassion. Amy sat back on the rail and swiped at her eyes. "Thanks, sweetie." She began to absently stroke the animal's back again, staring up at the sky. There were no stars and hardly any illumination, and she felt very alone. She kept stroking Desiree's back, contemplating why it seemed like nothing in life was easy. She liked Ira, she really did, but...

Biting down hard on the inside of her cheek, she struggled to force back a thought that kept trying to break into her consciousness. Fisting her hands at her cheeks, she squeezed her eyes tight. She was *not* falling in love with Beau Diablo! She was not! His kiss had *not* meant the moon and the stars to her! Besides, his contempt for her was so palpable, she was surprised she didn't keep hitting it head-on, like an invisible shield, whenever she got within ten feet of the man.

She was crazy to allow such a ludicrous idea to intrude on her thoughts, spoiling her sleep. It didn't matter that she melted when she saw him, that her heart tripped over itself at the sound of his voice. It didn't mean anything that even his grim expression thrilled her more than Ira's friendly laugh and ingratiating charm. Beau made it clear with every look, every word he spoke, that he didn't like her, and she was determined to keep that feeling completely mutual.

Deep inside her brain, a little voice nagged, *"Who are you trying to convince, Amy? Me—or you?"* The mental query shook her.

"What do you think, Desiree?" she whispered shakily. "Any answers?" She shook her head at herself. Here she was seeking advice from a three-day-old calf, in weather that would gleefully turn her to an ice sculpture in an hour's time. Was she going crazy or was she just lonely and nervous about getting married?

She remembered her mother confiding how frightened she'd been before her wedding, and how she'd almost run screaming into the street. But she hadn't, and years later she'd been able to smile at her daughter and say that she was glad she hadn't.

Taking a breath of icy air, she stood, giving the calf one last hug. "Thanks, honey. I think you're right." This quiet time out here with an accepting companion had helped clear her mind. What she needed to do was get to Diablo Butte and see Ira face-to-face. Have that talk. And if by some chance she felt he wasn't willing to try to make a real marriage, then she wouldn't go through with it.

If it came to that, she would figure out a way to deal with Mary's money problems. She knew, without a miracle, their medical debts were becoming insurmountable, but she wouldn't consider marrying someone for his money. If she did, she'd be as bad as Beau believed her to be.

Stepping back between the railing, she patted the calf's cheek. "You're a good little listener. Now get some sleep." The calf bawled and scooted up to stick its face through the fence, big eyes wistful. Amy gave in and hugged her again. "I guess you deserve a little extra loving, being awakened at three o'clock in the morning that way."

After kissing the calf on the top of its furry head, she hurried toward the ranch house. She was so cold she felt like a block of ice, and was grateful there would be coffee in the kitchen pot. Cookie always left some warming on winter nights for what she called "frost-bit cowboys".

After removing her parka, she checked the wall clock. It was just past three-thirty. Pouring herself a cup, she sat down before the kitchen fire. It didn't provide much warmth, and when she looked at it, she discovered there was nothing left but embers.

Resolved to find heat somewhere, she stood and pushed through the kitchen door, heading around the corner. Flickering light in the living room caught her eye, and she smiled. How nice. She could thaw out before a real fire. Silently blessing the person who'd put on logs too large to burn quickly away, she headed for the fireplace, settling on the wide stone lip of the outer hearth.

She sniffed the strong coffee, then sipped. It warmed her insides as the blaze caressed her back. Inhaling deeply, she savored the smell of the wood fire mingled with the coffee. She was learning to like this brawny Wyoming brew, and she was discovering she enjoyed spending quiet time like this. She only wished she didn't have such troublesome thoughts milling around in her brain, driving her insane with worry. Trying to push from her mind all her fears about Ira's motives and her uninvited attraction to Beau, she muttered, "I really, really *hate* this!"

"I'm sorry our coffee isn't up to your standards, Miss Vale."

Amy's head snapped up and she scanned the darkness. He wasn't on the couch or the nearby chairs. She could see them too well in the fire's glow. Hearing movement, she veered around to stare into the blackness at the back of the room. He must have been standing before the window wall, watching the night. Now she could see him, a vague silhouette, slightly blacker than the blackness of the shadowy world beyond. He was moving, coming nearer.

She set her mug aside, for it had begun to shake so violently she was afraid she'd drop it if she didn't. "D-don't you sleep?" Why did he—*of all people*—have to show up?

"Apparently I get as much sleep as you do." He came so close their boots almost touched. When he stopped, he shrugged his hands into his jeans pockets. "What are you doing prowling around at this hour?"

She couldn't tell if he was accusing her of anything or not. His tone gave nothing away. Presenting a cavalier attitude she didn't feel, she smirked. "I was casing the joint for pawnable stuff. You know, sterling silverware, gold jewelry, big wheels of cheese. The usual loot *bimbos* steal."

An ironic smile tugged at one corner of his mouth. "And you decided to take a break from stealing cheese and have some coffee?"

fling some hard truths at him, make him furious enough to keep his distance.

"I think you—you *want* me, Mr. Diablo." She eyed him directly, using all her willpower to keep her voice from cracking. "I think it irritates you that your father is marrying me—because—because you're hot for me and you can't have me!" She had no idea if what she was saying would truly make him mad or if he'd merely laugh at her and mock her the way he had so many times before. But she'd started this, so she had to plunge on, intent on making him despise the sight of her. "I think you want to kiss me right now, but you're trying to manipulate me—*the shallow party girl*—to start things for you so you don't have to betray your father. You want me to betray him for you. Well, I'm *not* the conniving snake here. You are. So, if you want a piece of my—my action, buddy, you have to do your own dirty work. And I don't believe even an egotistical jerk like you would sink that low." She clamped her jaws together and jumped to her feet. *There! If that didn't make him want to throw her off a cliff, she didn't know what would!*

She had only taken a step away from him when she found herself caught by the wrist. He was suddenly standing, growling out an oath. "*Dammit!*" He dragged her to face him, his features fierce. "You're right, Amy. I do want you. But you're wrong about my father." Taking her by the shoulders, he tugged her against him. "I don't give a damn about betraying him. He *invented* the word."

Amy's eyes stung with tears at his savage tone, but she blinked them back. "Let me go!"

"You don't want that. You want me as much as I want you."

She was dizzy with longing, but she tried to deny the truth. She opened her lips, but no angry rejection came. Suddenly, they were clinging together in a rush of wayward desire. Claiming her lips hungrily, he crushed her to him. The sensual ravishment of her mouth sent spirals of delight through her and she stood on tiptoe, hugging him, hating herself, but unable to push away. What he'd told her had been agonizingly on target. She wanted him as badly as he wanted her. His slightest touch set her aflame, burning away all her good intentions.

Moaning with desire, she returned his kisses with careless abandon, her hands searching, exploring his broad back. He felt so thrillingly male, his scent an aphrodisiac as his hands massaged an exciting message she couldn't ignore.

The demanding mastery of his kisses made her feel faint, and when his lips moved along her jaw and began to nip gently at her throat, she grew so light-headed with need she feared she would lose her ability to stand.

Just when she knew she would surely sink to the floor, he lifted her in his arms. "You're so beautiful." He kissed her temple. "I knew we'd be good together."

Drugged by his lovemaking, she allowed herself to be eased onto the couch. How welcome Beau's hard warmth was as he slid over her. She sighed, pressing her open lips to his, quivering with the hot intimacy of his kiss. Gathered against his firm torso, her body cried out for a deeper intimacy. As he inflamed her passion, she could feel his arousal grow and her senses reeled.

"You'll never marry my father," Beau muttered against her mouth.

Something in his ragged assertion caused the reasoning part of her brain to click on, setting off an alarm. Was there a tinge of satisfaction in his voice? What was going on here? What was she doing? How could she lose herself the way she had—like some mindless, amoral twit?

She was acting just the way Beau had expected her to act! A horrible idea struck. Was this seduction planned to pay his father back—betrayal for betrayal? Of course it was. Beau didn't even *like* her. What had possessed her to dare him with her own foolish lips? Did she really believe he wouldn't take her up on it? *She'd played right into his hands.* Now he would take satisfaction in reporting to Ira that his shallow, party-girl fiancée had cheated on him only days before the wedding—with his own son.

She moaned, sick at heart. Though her limbs were passion weakened and her body loath to comply, she slid her arms from around his neck and pressed impotently against his chest. "No..." she cried, but the only sound she heard was a fervent sigh. His hand was on her thigh, moving upward to breach the ribbing of her sweater. She gasped with involuntary delight as his seductive fingers dipped beneath the knit fabric to touch bare flesh. With all her flagging strength, she fought her hunger to surrender. "I—I'm not going to give you the satisfaction," she whimpered against his jaw. "Get off me!"

"Amy, you don't mean that." His hand had stilled, but he made no move to obey her. "Let me."

She closed her eyes, struggling for supremacy over her crazy need for him. "It's wrong. I wouldn't be able to forgive myself."

"Sex is natural." He caressed her throat with persuasive lips. "Don't fight it."

Every fiber in her body wanted those marvelous lips to dip lower but she resisted her craving, pushing hard. "Get—*up*!"

She thought she heard him groan, but she wasn't sure it was anything but a frustrated exhaling. "Amy—you don't love my father."

"That's between your father and me." She shoved harder against him. "Why should you care anyway?"

"I don't care." He lifted his face from hers, his jaw tight. But he didn't relinquish his intimate position. "I've told you I don't care."

"I think you do." She managed to conjure up a withering stare, though she felt drained, humiliated. "Oh—I don't mean you care about *me*. But I know you're full of rage about what your father did to your mother, and how he's lived his life since."

Beau's nostrils flared, and she thought she saw a flash of pain mix with the ire in his gaze.

Desperate to rid herself of the haunting feel of his kisses, she rubbed shaky fingers across her lips. It didn't help; the feeling lingered, torturing her. She was so miserable she had to strike back at him for his cruel, revengeful seduction. "You're so arrogant you think you know everything," she hissed. "Well, maybe you have a right to resent some things about Ira's past, but this time you're wrong. Your father has asked *nothing* of me but my companionship for as long as I want it that way."

For an endless moment, he watched her with sparking eyes. "Miss Vale," he finally ground out, "either you're very naive about what marriage is, or you think *I* am."

Before she could conjure up a scathing retort, he slid to her side. In a defensive move, she scrambled away. Far from steady on her feet, she leaned against the arm of the couch to collect herself.

He stood, too, every line of his body taut as if held still by ironfisted control. He shoved his hands into his pockets, and she had the feeling he would have grabbed her back into his arms if not for his conscious effort to resist. "You're still planning to go through with the marriage?" he asked.

"Of course!" Fury edged her words with ice, covering her breathlessness. She was so confused and hurt she didn't even stop to wonder if what she was saying was true anymore. Besides, Beau didn't deserve any open, honest admissions after what he'd done. "If your father still *wants* to marry me after you revenge yourself by reporting back what happened here tonight."

Fleetingly, a small, bitter smile twisted his lips. "I assume I don't have your vote for gentleman of the year, then?"

"What does that mean?"

His gaze slid to the fire as he clenched and unclenched his jaw. "Nothing happened here," he muttered.

Misery filled her heart at his gibe. It didn't matter that he was unaware of her love for him; it was just so hurtful that he could casually toss off what they'd shared as an unsuccessful means to an end.

Righteous indignation surged through her, strengthening her limbs and her resolve. "Why don't you go look at yourself in the mirror, Mr. Diablo?" Fighting tears, she pivoted away. "You might see some of the same imperfections you hate in your father in your *own* reflection!"

CHAPTER NINE

ONLY an inch of snow fell today, but the winds through Diablo Pass were howling up to forty miles an hour, piling more snow on the road and making visibility nonexistent. Beau had received reports that it would take at least two days of calm weather to clear the mounting drifts. This couldn't have been worse news for Amy.

She'd talked to Ira on the radio this evening after dinner. There were four cowhands in the bunkhouse at the time, as well as Beau's forbidding presence, so she could only chat about the weather, her newly acquired ranching skills and her growing affection for Wyoming. She didn't mention her blisters, her sore muscles or her scowling host. And once again, she was left with Ira's promise to repay her patience with that trip to France.

When she'd left the bunkhouse, she had a feeling everyone's eyes had been on her. She hadn't realized Beau's employees still didn't know she was Ira's fiancée and she sensed that they didn't think highly of the idea, though no one said anything. It was something in their eyes—a sort of disappointment in her—and it made her unaccountably sad. Clearly, Ira and his string of women weren't the most beloved people in this part of the state.

As she carried a pile of towels and clothes to the laundry room, she tried to shake off the realization. Work had always helped her forget her troubles

151

before. So she decided to let work do its job again. Besides, she'd never liked the idea of Cookie waiting on her hand and foot, and had no intention of allowing the housekeeper to increase her work load on her account. Doing laundry seemed like a good way to be helpful and to take her mind off Beau—er—the unrelenting *snow*.

Heading into the kitchen with her bundle, she found her mind drifting to thoughts about what had happened between Beau and her last night. Even all her activity couldn't seem to keep those heated memories at bay. Pulling her lips between her teeth, she recalled his admonition about how naive she was. She didn't want to believe it, but she was starting to realize she'd been naive about a lot of things, things that—because of her sister's needs—had blinded her to certain troublesome facts.

Now, that she'd had all day to stew on Beau's remark, she understood Ira would want more than simple companionship before too long. After all, he was only in his late fifties, a healthy man, with many good years left. And recently she'd discovered how very normal she was—with all the needs and desires of any woman. How ironic that she'd learned that truth from a man who disliked her so intensely.

She knew now, if she planned to keep her marriage to Ira platonic, she would ultimately be cheating them both. Besides, how could she offer him anything more than companionship after what she'd learned these past few days? She didn't love him. And having met his son, she feared she never could feel anything more for him than mild affection.

Mindlessly, she opened the door to the steamy laundry room where at least one of the washing machines and two commercial-size dryers were sloshing and whirring all day long. Loading up another of the washers with her things, she reluctantly let her mind roam along dark, worrisome paths she could no longer avoid.

What if Ira *had* been making empty promises, playing on her trusting nature and her weakness for Mary, just to get himself another young plaything? If so, it would be better this way, breaking it off before it got worse. On the other hand, could Beau be deliberately making trouble, manipulating her to doubt her own motives and Ira's? If that was the case, then she would be hurting Ira badly by breaking their engagement. She hated the thought. The last thing she wanted was to hurt anyone, but she really had no choice—not after tasting Beau's sizzling kisses.

She added bleach and soap and turned on the machine, hardly registering her actions. Her mind rebuked, *"How could you have gotten yourself into such a mess?"* She supposed her mental state when she'd met Ira had been greatly to blame. She'd been weary of the sleazy passes she received every night from drunks who thought they were God's gift to womankind. And she'd been worried sick about her sister's upcoming surgery and the ever-present bills. Ira had been so kind, such a respectful gentleman. And he'd made her laugh. When he'd proposed, it had seemed like the perfect answer to all her predicaments.

Beau was right. She had been naive. The only difference was, he'd made the remark sarcastically. He didn't truly believe she was naive. There was no doubt in her mind that he thought she was using Ira for his money and lying to Beau to appease him.

She left the kitchen and hurried through the living room, working to stave off mental images of what had happened there last night. Turning down the long hall that headed away from her room, she made for the linen closet to retrieve clean towels.

Her mind spiraled back to Mary, and she swiped at a tear. It was all so painfully clear now. She'd acted impetuously, not carefully considering what her marriage to Ira would be like. And adding guilt upon guilt, she finally had to admit to herself that her concern over Mary had been the major reason she'd so abruptly accepted Ira's proposal.

She felt vile about that. If that wasn't enough, she now knew she would be carrying around the memory of a pair of furious blue eyes for a very long time.

Reaching the linen-closet door, she made a vow to herself. She would keep a brave face until the weather cleared. Then she would travel to Ira's ranch and break off her engagement. She owed Ira the courtesy of telling him face-to-face. It would be unfair just to run away. The specter of Mary's medical bills rose before her like a threatening demon, and she shuddered with dismay. Still, she couldn't allow money to sway her any longer. She refused to believe she could be the sort of woman Beau thought she was.

Swinging open the door, she froze in a stunned tableau, her hands outstretched toward shelves that weren't there. Her lips parted in horror. Clearly, she'd opened the wrong door. Instead of a linen closet, she found herself standing in the entryway of a bathroom, a simple, well-lit cubicle, its foggy air fragrant with the scent of soap. A few scant steps in front of her, Beau stood, clad only in a towel.

Her heart stopped as he paused in the act of shaving, a straight razor hovering along his jaw. He was so striking, towering there in his near nudity. His well-muscled chest, silky with dark hair, glistened with moisture from his shower, and his long, sturdy legs were braced wide. The saddle muscles were clearly defined in his powerful thighs. She watched them flex as he shifted, and a tingle of excitement danced along her spine as she recalled how delightfully firm they'd felt beneath her hips.

For some reason, she couldn't back away and close the door. She just stood rooted there like a potted plant, gaping. With the lift of an inquiring brow, he canted his head her way. "Is this a come-on, or were you hoping to see me slit my throat?"

"*Oh*! I—I'm sorry," she stuttered. "I was looking for a towel...."

With a roguish twitch of his lips, he tucked a thumb inside the one tied at his waist and tugged. "If you need one that badly—take mine."

The flash of bare, taut hip knocked her out of her paralysis. Fumbling for the knob, she managed to slam the door a second before his towel thudded against it.

Rich, mocking laughter chased her down the hall.

Snow, snow and more snow! The next day was an exhausting carbon copy of so many before, and Amy was tired. But before she fell into bed, she decided to look in on Desiree. The innocent little calf always lifted her spirits. And now that her future was so bleak and insecure, she found herself visiting Desiree more and more.

Though the cowboys were friendly and respectful, they seemed distant, knowing she was engaged to Ira. She felt bad about that. Even so, she didn't intend to defensively blurt out that she wasn't going to marry him after all. Ira deserved to hear it from her first.

After a quiet visit, she gave Desiree a melancholy hug. "Good night, sweetie. I promise, after I leave here, I'll write." She stood, then realized what she'd said and laughed at herself, even in her dour mood. "Well, maybe not *write*. But since we're so good at mental telepathy, I'll 'think' my love to you. Okay?"

The calf blinked and bawled.

"Then it's settled. After I leave, I'll think to you every day." Turning away, she waved at the calf, feeling a new surge of depression. She would have to leave her little pet behind when she returned to Chicago. She had a feeling her landlord's "no pets" rule probably included cows. "Get some sleep, sweetie." The sadness in her voice startled her. This place had gotten into her blood awfully quickly. *"Not just the place,"* her brain jeered. She bit down hard on her lip, hoping the pain would make her forget *who* had gotten into her blood since her coming out here.

She trudged around the calving barn toward the ranch house, noticing the snow had stopped and the wind that had blown insistently all day had died. She looked up. There were even a few brave stars twinkling down at her.

Off in the distance, she heard the crunch of hooves on frozen snow. Turning toward the sound, she squinted through the dimness, focusing on a stand of pines. In the dusk, she saw a man on horseback emerging from the woods.

Her heart lurched when she realized it was Beau astride his black stallion. As he drew nearer, she could see his brows were frosted silver and he was wearing a dark bandanna over his mouth and nose. For a split second, she was transported back in time—to a lawless era where even the best of men could be wild and dangerous if driven far enough. Right now, Amy couldn't think of any man, anywhere, more threatening to her peace of mind than the one before her now.

The horse stilled under Beau's wordless command, and for a long moment they watched each other. He reached up and yanked his kerchief down, revealing a grim smile that hid nothing of his smoldering antagonism. He startled her when he signaled his horse forward. She didn't move, and wasn't sure why she didn't, for he was heading directly at her.

Lifting her chin, she eyed him grudgingly. She didn't want to be spellbound, standing helplessly in the subzero night, breathless to see what he was planning. But for some reason, she couldn't bear the idea of leaving, never to know what was on his mind.

When he reached her, he brought the stallion to a halt and held out a gloved hand, as though there was no question that she'd accept it and allow herself to be lifted into his lap. *How audacious of him*! *How dare he*? Yet even as she mentally berated him, finding him the most arrogant, egotistical rogue in the world, she lifted her arms, welcoming his invitation.

In the wink of an eye, he swung her up into the saddle, her legs straddling his thighs. Though she snuggled against him, she was shocked at herself for allowing this to happen. It couldn't have been a worse time to discover she no longer had the strength to fight her attraction for him. These days and nights of imprisonment with him had broken her resolve until it was nothing more than tattered, useless threads.

He steered his stallion away from the light, leading them toward the darkened wood. For a long time, Sovereign walked among the snow-laden pine boughs, the only sounds his hoofbeats in the snow and the occasional creak of leather. Amy didn't know where they were going and didn't care. She inhaled the cold air, Beau's warm scent mingling with it, stirring the embers of her passion. She squeezed her eyes shut, praying she wouldn't betray herself tonight, but far from sure of anything anymore.

After a long, quiet ride, they emerged on a bluff overlooking a wide, open valley. After the darkness of the wood, the clearing night and luminous snow seemed almost as bright as day. Amy blinked, taking a slow sweep of the idyllic scene. In the valley's center, a teardrop lake glimmered like a dusky jewel. Within the depths of the frozen water winked reflected stars from the Wyoming heavens, like diamonds set in the lake floor.

Beau didn't say a word, just led his steed along the bluff above the Christmas-card lake. The setting was so charming and unspoiled, Amy couldn't speak even if she'd wanted to. They rode along in the white silence, and she found herself wishing she had the slightest urge to be anywhere else in the world. But, sadly, she didn't.

After a time, Beau reined in his horse, and she felt him move, tilt back his Stetson and gaze into the sky. She heard him inhale, but he said nothing. Unable to stand the suspense, she worked to gather the remnants of her wits. "Do you have some ice that needs chopping?'' she asked, trying to make light of her loss of control. His chuckle tingled through her, giving her a guilty sense of pleasure. *This wasn't helping!* She tried again. ''Is there a cow that's slipped on the ice and you need me to lift him up?''

''I didn't realize you could lift cows, Miss Vale.''

His tone was teasing, and she tried to be affronted, but she wasn't in the mood to fight. Far from it. ''Try me.'' She flinched. That challenge had come out more like a sexual invitation than a test of her cow-lifting skills. She had to get ahold of herself. Grabbing the saddle horn, she shifted forward. ''Where are we going, then? Are you planning to murder me and dump me in that sinkhole?''

''Maybe later.'' His warm breath ruffled her hair. Using his free arm, he coaxed her back against him, cutting off her renewed vow to keep an emotional distance. She settled there, regretfully accepting the terrible knowledge that she was his—body and soul. Defeat shrouded her heart. She had no more strength to escape him, and tragically, she had no desire to.

With the boundless winter stillness as their companion, he led his steed farther into the storybook valley. ''Take a deep breath,'' he murmured. ''That's the perfume of snow on the sage.''

She did as he asked, catching his stirring scent in the bargain. The combination was mellow and stimulating. Though she reacted inwardly with a wanton shiver, she managed to remain outwardly composed. Even so, words failed her.

''I wanted you to experience the Wyoming I love.''

She sensed his scorn and frowned. ''You really don't believe I could appreciate the beauty of all this?''

"I don't think you can appreciate anything but a dollar sign."

She stiffened, pulling away. "You can't mean that! Surely you've found out *that* much about me!"

"I think your motives are possibly less grasping than I'd first thought, but marrying someone because of medical bills doesn't take you out of the bimbo category, and you know it."

"So you've figured that out, have you?" she snapped, stung by his accusation. Struggling from his arms, she managed to jump from the saddle. "Congratulations, Inspector Clouseau! You've nabbed your bimbo!" She tumbled into the snow, floundering to her knees. "Just for the record, I love Wyoming, I love my sister and—"

"And what?" he demanded, suddenly there, his hands gripping her arms.

She grappled to keep him from helping her, but couldn't extricate herself from his grasp. Jamming her fists against him, she fought not only his sensual pull but her inner turmoil. She wasn't the cheap sort of woman he thought she was. But what could she do—blurt out her love for him? That would be quite a sight—his amused expression at the conquest of his father's fiancée. That would kill her soul.

"And *nothing*!" she retorted. "I keep telling you, what's between your father and me is none of your business!"

She tried to jerk from his hold, but only succeeded in falling on her back. His strength was too much for her and she couldn't evade him. They were lying in the snow, Beau above her. His mouth set, he demanded coldly, "Admit you're *not* in love."

Dismay washed through her. How could she admit that? She was in love—only *not* with Ira, but with a man who didn't trust her, didn't believe a word she said. "I can't admit that!" She told the sad truth contemptuously, in an effort to mask her heartbreak. "Because I *am* in love." Their breaths mingled in charged air. She wanted to hold him, kiss him, love him right here in the snow. But knowing it would be a fool's errand to start anything that could only lead to heartbreak, she grabbed at the snow to keep from taking him in her arms. With heavy sadness in her heart, she demanded, "*Happy* now?"

His gaze held all the warmth of a block of granite. "Ecstatic." Suddenly, he lowered angry lips to hers. She gasped at the blistering effect of his mouth against hers, and her resistance melted like a snowflake in a volcano. She moved to take him in her desperate embrace, to return fiery kiss for fiery kiss. But before she could even lift her arms, he cursed against her lips, flinging himself away.

Shaken and aching for more, she lay there staring up at him as he yanked off his Stetson and jerked a hand through his hair. She was astonished to discover he was gentleman enough to be ashamed of himself for kissing an engaged woman who'd just confessed she was in love—though he was wrong about *whom* she loved.

Oddly, she realized she was no longer ashamed of herself for wanting him to kiss her, or even angry with him for mistrusting her. On the contrary, lying here on her back in the snow, she felt thoroughly alive. How devious life could be.

He stood and swatted his hat against his jeans, dusting off snow in quick, angry strokes. Not sure why she wanted to communicate with him, but positive she must, she struggled up on an elbow. "For your information, I think Wyoming in winter is lovely, too. I'm not exactly the Wicked Witch of the West, you know."

He glanced at her. For an instant, his eyes seemed to flash with the rage and pain of a wounded animal, but the look was gone so quickly, Amy decided her dazed mind was playing tricks on her.

"Forget it," he growled. "Go live your life. I'll stay out of it from now on." Stooping, he took her arm, hoisting her to her feet. "I'll help you into the saddle."

She stared at him. "Aren't you—"

"I need to walk."

After boosting her on his horse, he grabbed the reins, leading them back toward civilization. Taking a deep, unsteady breath, she watched him hike through the snow with long, irascible strides.

Strangling the saddle horn, she battled to keep from bursting into tears. Why did she have to discover love was real in this horrible way? And why did she have to learn that the soft emotion was not necessarily returned?

She loved Beau Diablo with all her heart—a man committed to his land, admired by his employees and friends and true to his word. She had a strong sense that when the right woman came along, he would be totally committed to her, too. Unfortunately, he thought Amy Vale was the most *wrong* female to ever walk the face of the earth.

She knew it would do no good to tell him how she felt. He would only laugh, unable to trust anything she said, unable to believe she could actually love him—not after coming out here to marry his father.

He would simply think she'd discovered through idle ranch chatter that he was a wealthier—and therefore *better*—meal ticket.

She fought her need to slip from the saddle, run to him, pull him down in the snow and savor the full heat and depth of his passions, no matter how fleeting her joy might be. She was a coward and couldn't bear to witness his dry grin of vengeance once it was done. So she simply stared after him, hopeless longing shimmering in her eyes.

Two days passed as the weather gradually cleared. The phone lines to Diablo Butte were repaired, and the bulldozers were making headway clearing the pass. Amy's heart was torn with a need to leave Beau's ranch and a tormenting desire to stay—even if she had to endure blisters and angry glowers forever. She knew that was crazy and impractical. Ever since their rash tumble in the snow, Beau had kept a distance. Every time their eyes met, his glances were stormy and brooding.

Amy finished lunch in the cook house. So far today, she hadn't seen Beau, so it startled her when he called her name. She shifted toward the side door where he'd just entered. Before she could speak, he said, "Ira's on the phone for you."

A knot tightened in her stomach, but she stood, nodding.

"You can take it in my den."

Refusing to meet his malevolent gaze, she grabbed her coat and darted outside.

As she rushed into the kitchen, she spied the wall phone and decided to take the call there. Everybody was in the cook house. And she didn't feel like facing

Beau's den. She knew it was down the hall from his room, but entering his personal sanctuary would be more agonizing than worthwhile. She lifted the receiver and worked on sounding cheerful "Hello, Ira."

"Hello, little one," he bellowed through a laugh. "You sound fine. I'm surprised. I thought you'd be sick with a cold after all the work my slave-driver son made you do."

She ducked her head, her gaze sliding to the floor. "No, I'm just fine." She wanted to say she'd enjoyed being out in the snow, laughing and joking with the men, warming her insides with coffee strong enough to support a cow all by itself. She liked the feeling of accomplishment at the end of the day. She'd certainly never felt fulfilled after a night at the bar.

"The road's almost cleared, little one. Boy, I can't wait to see you," he was saying. "I have a special dinner waiting. French champagne's on ice, too." Amy flinched. He sounded excited—like a bridegroom. "I figure we can get the preacher out here tomorrow and make it official."

"Official . . ." She echoed the word, a bad feeling creeping up her spine. Why did she sense that he was planning on starting the marriage *unofficially* tonight—in a very carnal way. "Uh—Ira—I need to talk to you about something that's very important—"

"Sure, little one. We can do anything you want."

She anxiously twisted the phone cord around a finger. He was appeasing her, not really listening. "Ira," she whispered, "I'm not quite packed. Maybe I'd better go finish."

"Great. Great." He laughed again. "Don't want to have you get here one second later than you have to."

"Okay. Well—bye."

"Love you, little one." He made a kissing sound in the phone. "Now get here as soon as you can."

"I—I will." She heard a click in her ear, signaling that he'd hung up. Feeling suddenly very contaminated, she needed to talk to her sister and dialed the number for the convalescent home. It rang only two times before it was answered.

"Hello? This is Amy Vale. May I speak to my sister, please?"

The operator said the usual "One moment," before she was put on hold.

"Hello, Miss Vale?" came a nasal male voice.

"Yes?"

"This is Dr. Rampling."

He sounded jovial, so she assumed he must have left instructions to put her on for an update the next time she called. "Oh, hi, Dr. Rampling. Everything okay?"

"Splendid. I just wanted to let you know how much we appreciate the payment your fiancé made. It covers Mary's bills up to now, and includes an advance for next month. That should take her right up until time to travel."

The knot in Amy's stomach constricted, and she leaned weakly against the wall. "Oh? I—he didn't mention it."

"Well, I won't keep you talking. Mary is coming along very well. I believe with this last surgery, she'll be walking without a limp before too long."

Tears of joy welled in her eyes. "Oh, Doctor, I've waited five years to hear that. Thank you—" Her voice broke. "Thank you so much."

"It was your sister's courage that got her this far. Here, I'll transfer you to her room."

"Thank you, Doctor, and once again I want to—" Before she could finish speaking, he was gone. She shook her head at his disinclination to accept thanks. When she heard Mary's voice, her spirits soared.

They talked for a quarter of an hour, and Mary's lightheartedness made Amy laugh several times. Yet deep in her heart she knew she had to tell her sister the truth. Finally, Mary asked, "What is it, Amy? You sound—funny."

Eyeing the ceiling, Amy sighed. She should have known. Mary didn't miss much. "Er—look, honey, I'm really sorry to have to tell you this, but I don't think I can go through with marrying Ira."

There was a pause of a few heartbeats before Mary said, "Good."

Amy was taken off guard. "Why good?"

"You didn't love him. Isn't that enough reason?"

Amy smiled wanly, feeling as though a weight had been lifted from her shoulders. "You knew?"

"Yeah. But I figured it was your business who you married."

"But Mom was happy, and she didn't love Dad when they got married."

"Ira isn't Dad."

Amy frowned, then realized Mary's simple statement had been terribly insightful. She laughed then. It wasn't much of a laugh, but it was a beginning. "You only talked to him on the phone one time. How did you get to be so wise?"

"I'm your sister, that's how," Mary insisted. "Now, come home as soon as you can. We'll make out. Why, in a month I'll be fine and I can get a job, too."

Amy's mood plummeted. "Don't you worry about getting a job, young lady. Just think about getting well."

"I love you, Amy. I can't wait to see you."

She heard a squeak and knew the kitchen door was opening. "I can't wait to see you either, honey. I love you. Bye."

She turned to hang up the receiver and was startled to see Beau, not Cookie, as she'd expected.

By some sort of ironic retribution, he appeared very much the same as he had the first moment she'd seen him—his Stetson brim pulled low over sparking eyes, that split-hide coat snug across wide shoulders. Anger curved his lips now, just as it had then. Only she hadn't been in love with him then—or maybe she had, even at that first crazy instant he'd stalked into the store.

"How is my father?" he asked.

Jarred from her dark musing, she realized he assumed she'd been on the phone with her fiancé all the time. "He's fine," she said minimally. What did it matter now? Soon she'd be on a bus to Chicago and she'd never see Beau again. "I—I was just about to finish packing."

"Good." He hung up his coat and tossed his hat onto one of the hooks. "The road to Diablo Butte is open."

Amy had the peculiar notion there was something behind the scorn in his words. Was it a touch of melancholy? Surely not. She shook off the fantasy. "I—guess I'd better get ready, then."

He nodded, his glance flicking her way for an instant. The quick, sharp look was like a knife in her soul. "When you're ready, Snapper will drive you."

Before she could say thank-you or even goodbye, he disappeared through the kitchen door. As his footsteps faded in the distance, her throat closed and she found it hard to catch her breath. The man she loved had just cavalierly walked away, making it brutally clear he didn't care to see her—ever again.

CHAPTER TEN

THE general store in Big Elk was brightly lit and practically empty. Ira's ranch hand who had given her a ride to the bus stop had dropped her off over an hour ago, and the bus wouldn't be arriving for another hour.

Amy turned the little book display, wishing she had enough money to buy a paperback novel. The trip back would be long and she desperately wished she had something to take her mind off this fateful trip out west.

In her mind's eye, she saw Ira's face when she'd told him she couldn't go through with the marriage. He'd pursed his lips and shaken his head, saying, "You can't be serious."

She had only been able to nod, fearful of how he would react when he realized she meant it. But he'd been civil, though he clearly wasn't happy. He'd even waved off her offer to pay him back for Mary's bills and insisted on giving her money for the bus. Still, she'd sworn she would repay him a little every month until the debt was settled.

She didn't blame him for leaving her to eat a silent, self-conscious dinner with his cowhands, and for assigning his testy old cook to show her to a guest room for the night. The same grumpy, toothless man had driven her to the bus stop this morning, grumbling to himself most of the way. Ira had come by this morning as she was eating breakfast and given an offhand wave, mouthing wishes that she have a good trip back, but he hadn't stopped to visit or ask how she'd slept. That hadn't surprised her. After all, he *had* been dumped. He probably felt he had a right to make her a little uncomfortable if he wanted to.

She had a feeling both his pride and his ego would soon heal, for the last thing he'd told her before he ambled out of the kitchen was that he planned to go to Houston, Texas in a couple of weeks for a cattlemen's meeting. She could already see plans for a new conquest gleaming in his eyes.

She browsed through the paperback novels, not really seeing the titles. The metal rack squawked as she turned it, the sound like a shriek in the empty store. She had her Wyoming textbook in her suitcase, but she couldn't stand the thought of reading about a place she'd grown to love but would never see again.

"Lady?"

Amy jumped at the unexpectedness of the store owner's voice. Since she was the only person in the place, he had to be speaking to her. "Yes?" She spun his way.

He grinned bashfully, and she remembered those big horse teeth. "I got some used books over here. These old *Star Trek* novels are only a dime each."

She colored. How did he know she couldn't afford a new book? She dropped her gaze to her suitcase, mortified. "No, thanks—I—I was just passing the time until the bus going east comes by."

"Sure—okay..." he mumbled, sounding embarrassed. She felt for him. He'd only been trying to do her a kindness. He probably kept old books under the counter for down-in-the-mouth wayfarers, charging a small price just to protect their pride.

The truth was, she didn't even have a dime to spare. Though she'd reluctantly accepted the ticket money from Ira, she'd refused to be indebted to him for a penny more. Edging away from the book rack, she self-consciously wound her hands together, trying to melt into the background. Bumping into a shelf below the front window, she decided to pass the time reading the sayings printed on the side of the souvenir mugs. Some of the phrases were off-color, but most were funny. She picked up one cup at a time, looking at each picture then reading its quotation. A few times, she almost smiled.

"Well, hon, I'm more surprised to see you than I would be to find a rattlesnake in my petticoats!"

Amy recognized Cookie's croaking voice and jerked around, nearly dropping the mug she was reading. "Oh...hello..." Apprehensive, she scanned the store to see if the housekeeper was alone. When she realized Beau wasn't with her, she let out a long breath, not sure if the sigh was one of relief or depression. Trying not to think about which it might be, she straightened her shoulders, working to appear casual.

"What in Sam Hill are you doing here?" Cookie absently handed the store owner a list. "Get me this stuff, will ya, Bud?" Before the portly man could respond, she'd turned back to Amy. "And when you find it all, go ahead and stick it in the back of the pickup. I want to gossip with my friend over here."

"Are—are you alone?" Amy asked, unable to help herself.

Cookie nodded, pulling off her knit cap, her flyaway hair popping out in all directions. She stuffed the cap in her coat pocket. "The dang thing's warm, but it itches." She grinned, though her eyes held more inquisitiveness than pleasure. "Now what are you doin' hanging around this ol' dump?" She waved off the proprietor's objection with a laugh, adding, "Is Mr. Ira dragging you in here to fetch supplies on your *honeymoon*?"

Amy shook her head, wondering why fate insisted on one more humiliation. Replacing the mug on the shelf, she stared out at the late-morning brightness. Sunshine glistened off the snow. Everything looked polished and gleaming and pure. How ironic that the most glorious day she'd experienced in Wyoming would not only be her last, but her saddest.

"Where is Mr. Ira anyway? Over at the gas station gabbing with Pete?"

"Cookie..." She faltered, unable to meet the older woman's eyes. "Ira and I aren't getting married after all."

When Cookie didn't speak, she found she had to see her expression, and shifted her gaze. "I'm afraid I made a mistake when I said I would marry him, and I decided it wouldn't work out."

Cookie's eyes were as big as saucers. "You told Mr. Ira *no*?"

Amy shrugged unhappily. "I had to. I found out I was—" She stopped herself, thinking better of what she'd almost revealed. "I guess I'm not cut out to be a rancher's wife after all."

Cookie pursed her lips, frowning. "Well, I can't say I'm sorry you ain't gonna marry Mr. Ira. That ol' maverick will find himself another filly soon enough." She put a friendly hand on Amy's arm. "So, what are you going to do?"

"Go back to Chicago. The doctor said Mary will be fine in a month. We'll get by."

Cookie nodded. "I sure wish you all the luck, hon, but I think you're wrong about one thing. You'd make a good rancher's wife."

Amy smiled sadly, then had a thought and her smile died. "Look, Cookie—" she took the housekeeper's arms in a pleading gesture "—don't tell Beau. Promise?"

The older woman gave her such a piercing, thorough look Amy was afraid she might detect the awful truth in her eyes. Hurriedly releasing the woman, she turned away, pretending to hunt for just the right souvenir mug.

After a long, strained minute, Cookie said, "Why would I tell that old grouch a thing?" She sounded oddly chipper, and Amy couldn't imagine why. "Mr. Beau ain't done nothin' but growl at everybody lately—like an ol' grizzly bear with a toothache." She harrumphed. "Ain't never seen him so cantankerous. Near bit my head off last night, and all I did was ask him if he wanted me to send your gloves over to Diablo Butte with one of the cowpokes. He near jumped down my throat. Grabbed 'em up. Said he'd handle it. Sorry. If I'da known you was going to be here, I'da brought 'em."

Amy unconsciously rubbed her cold hands together. The gloves had never entered her mind. "Don't worry about them—"

"Shucks, hon." She pulled off her worn leather gloves. "You take these. What if your bus got stuck. You could get mighty cold. Besides, I got me a ton of gloves."

"No—"

"Shush now," she admonished, thrusting them into
Amy's fingers. "Call it a thank-you gift for all your
help this past week."

Embarrassed, Amy accepted the gloves and slipped
them on, silently vowing to mail them back after she
got to Chicago. "Thanks. I appreciate it." She picked
up a mug, feigning interest in it. "And you will
promise you won't mention seeing me to Beau?"

"Sure, sure, hon. He won't hear nothin' from these
lips."

Amy lowered the mug, relieved. "Thanks." She
faced the woman again. Unable to help herself, she
hugged her. "I'll miss you."

"Shucks," Cookie said gently. "A tough old piece
of jerky like me?" She patted Amy's shoulder.
"That's a real sweet lie, hon. Real sweet."

"Got your stuff packed in the pickup," Bud called,
his pudgy face florid from the chore. The women separated after one more affectionate squeeze. "Cookie,
do you want me to put this load of supplies on Beau's
bill or would you rather pay cash and close out your
account? That way you can truck your grub in from
someplace that ain't such a dump."

Cookie guffawed. "Send the bill to Mr. Beau the
same as always, and quit lookin' so hangdog, you
fool." She slung an arm about the man's slumped
shoulders. "Okay. What if my next trip in I bring you
a pound of my pecan fudge? Will that square me with
ya?"

His puckered features cleared. "For your fudge, I'd
forgive you if you burned down this dump."

They both laughed. At the door, Cookie turned to
Amy and gave her a wink. "You know, hon, I have

a real strong feelin' things are going to work out for you."

Amy waved, forcing a smile. "Goodbye, Cookie..." Her voice broke with regret, and she couldn't say more. The door banged shut as Bud left with the housekeeper to escort her to the pickup.

The feeble rein Amy had on her emotions suddenly gave way and she sagged against the shelf. Her eyes were open but unseeing as a forlorn tear escaped down her cheek.

The bus was late, finally arriving at nearly one o'clock in the afternoon. Amy was tired and hungry, but she'd been tired and hungry before and she knew it wasn't fatal. One other passenger had arrived about fifteen minutes before the bus came, and Amy had the feeling Ira had been a bit vindictive, dropping her off so early. Apparently the bus was routinely late.

The motor coach was far from full, with plenty of empty seats, but the last thing she wanted was to be alone with her thoughts. She took a seat beside a young redhead about her age. The woman was extremely slender, with a sharp nose and big, wide-set hazel eyes, her lips full and wide. Amy decided with the right lighting and makeup, the thin woman could be a fashion model. The only flaw in the picture was the huge wad of gum she was chewing openmouthed. But Amy didn't care. The girl looked pleasant and might provide enough distraction to ease her aching heart.

"Hi," she said, after she'd stowed her suitcase on the overhead rack. "I hope you don't mind if I join you."

The redhead pulled a long, stringy ribbon of gum out of her mouth, then stuck it back, smiling all the while. "Hey, sit! I've been bored stiff." She shook out her red curls, running an emaciated hand through them. "I'm from Los Angeles. On my way to visit my boyfriend in Chicago. He's in graduate school there."

"I live there," Amy said, delighted she'd have a traveling companion for the entire trip.

"Cool." The girl snapped her gum, then held out her hand. "Name's Milly Koontz."

"Amy Vale." She accepted the girl's hand.

"Nice to meet you." She cast a glance out the window. "Pretty country around here."

Amy followed her gaze, feeling a wave of melancholy as she watched white-clad hills roll by. A knot formed in her throat. "Yes—it is...." she whispered.

"What were you doing out here? Visiting friends?"

Amy felt flushed and hoped she wasn't blushing with distress. Forcing herself to relax, she lay back against the seat, avoiding her seatmate's eyes. "Sort of..." Wanting to change the subject, she asked, "Where's your boyfriend studying?"

"Northwestern."

She felt another pang. Attending Northwestern had been another dream she'd seen slip through her fingers. "It's a fine school," she murmured. "What's he studying?"

"*Giddyap, stud-a-rama!*"

Amy grimaced in confusion. What sort of graduate course was that? She shifted to look at Milly. "I've never heard of giddy—whatever. Is it a foreign language or something?" Milly seemed not to hear, something outside the bus having caught her attention. Nudging her seatmate, Amy asked, "What sort of graduate course is your boyfriend in?"

Milly came back with a start. "Huh? Oh, Vernon? He's a classical flautist, working on a master's degree in music. I was talking about that cowboy out there." She pointed toward the horizon, dotted with pine and fur trees. "Is he a total *stud* or what?"

Amy didn't see anyone from her vantage point, but when the bus chugged around a turn, she saw the object of Milly's admiration. A horseman atop a black stallion galloped along a ridge. The horse was throwing up great clouds of snow as it plunged across the range, its muscles pumping and straining, nostrils blowing frosty air.

"I wonder where he's racing?"

Amy watched the approaching cowboy with a sense of disbelief. He looked awfully familiar, but of course that was impossible.

"He seems to be racing the bus," Milly said, echoing the conjecture of several other passengers who'd also spotted the rider's approach.

Something swelled in her throat, something she didn't even want to think of as hope. She tamped the emotion down. First of all, it couldn't possibly be Beau, and even if it was, it was a coincidence that he was here. He wasn't racing the bus, for heaven's sake.

"Wow," Milly whispered. "He's *gorgeous*."

Amy stared, afraid to even think. The bus had rounded another curve, and the cowboy was now heading straight for them. He'd taken off his black Stetson and was waving it at the driver.

"Stop the bus," a woman shouted. "That guy wants on."

"Not with no horse, he's not getting on," the driver complained.

"Maybe he's going to rob us!" a bespectacled woman whined. "I've heard of that sort of thing out here in the West."

"That was a hundred years ago, Mabel," the woman's portly husband rebuked. "The guy doesn't even have a gun."

"You don't know that. It could be hidden in his jeans!"

"I'll check for suspicious bulges," Milly cracked with a wicked chuckle.

"Stop the bus," another passenger shouted. Amy craned around to look at him. He was the middle-aged man wearing Western clothes who'd gotten on the bus with Amy, so he must be from the area. "That's Beau Diablo. Owns one of the biggest spreads in the state. He ain't gonna rob us. Maybe he needs help."

The argument went on, but Amy didn't hear it. Her mind was reeling with such a wild mixture of hope and dread, she couldn't think straight. What did Beau want with this bus? Surely he didn't need to get rid of her gloves so badly he'd race cross-country to personally toss them in her face.

"Anybody know why this man wants me to stop my bus?" the driver asked over his loudspeaker.

Amy swallowed hard, but couldn't answer.

"He's shouting something," Milly said, sliding her window open.

"*Dammit, Amy, tell him to stop the bus!*"

"*Amy?*" Milly asked, twirling to her new friend. "Is that you?"

"I—I'm not sure," she hedged.

Milly pulled up on her knees, sticking her head out the window. "Amy *who?*" she yelled.

"*Vale!*"

Milly plopped down in the seat, staring at Amy. "Is that gorgeous hunk the 'sort of' friend you were visiting? And if he is, why are you *leaving?*"

"He hates me," she mumbled. "He probably decided to give me a bill for my room and board, that's all."

"Stop the damn bus," shouted the man who'd recognized Beau. "If you don't, he's going to jump off that horse and kill himself trying to get on."

"Oh, let him jump!" Milly cried, her eyes alight. "I bet he can make it."

Amy hid her head in her hands, scandalized.

"Hell," the driver groused. "This ain't in the manual."

"He's going to do it! He's going to jump!" Mabel cried. "Speed up. He'll murder us all."

"Shut up, woman," her husband snapped. "No more caffeine for you. It makes you nuts."

Beau had moved up alongside the bus and was pounding on the door, demanding that it be opened. By now, the general chant was "*Stop the bus! Stop the bus!*" *The only people not joining in were Mabel and Amy.*

"*Crap!*" the driver groused. Pulling the lever, he opened the front door with a whoosh.

Amid gasps and applause, Beau leaped off his panting stallion and onto the vehicle.

"Stop this damned thing," Beau growled.

Milly groaned. "Shoot! I swallowed my gum!" But Amy hardly registered her choked complaint. She couldn't take her eyes off the furious man towering down the aisle in front of her, dwarfing the vehicle with his angry presence.

When his sparking eyes fell on his quarry, they narrowed dangerously. "One of your passengers took something of mine and I intend to get it back."

The initial shock of Beau's appearance was wearing off, and she found herself overcome by a wave of black, unreasoning anger. Why had Cookie broken her word? And what had she done that had been so unforgivable that would make Beau go to such lengths to disgrace her one final time?

Milly poked Amy's ribs. "What did you take from this guy, the Hope diamond?"

"I didn't take anything. He just hates me."

He stalked over to her and scooped her up, depositing her unceremoniously over a shoulder. She was so disoriented by being treated like a sack of feed, she didn't even struggle as he turned around and headed toward the door.

"Wow!" Milly heaved a breathy sigh. "When Tarzan's through hating you, tell him he can hate me!"

"You can't take that woman off the bus, mister!" the driver yelled.

Beau jerked around to scowl at the scrawny man. "Are *you* going to stop me?"

The driver's head seemed to shrink into his shoulders with Beau's intimidating stare. "Uh—well, I guess it's none of my business. Just get off with her quick. I got my schedule, you know."

Beau carted her down the steps to the roadside. Amy registered the fact that the bus's engines were revving up, and it snapped her out of her stupefaction. "I didn't take anything of yours! Let me down!'' She pounded on his back. "That's my bus!"

"Not anymore, it's not."

She wriggled to get free, but without success. "You—you can't *kidnap* me!"

"Weren't you paying attention, Miss Vale?" He began to trudge toward his horse. "I just did."

"Yooohooo!"

She veered toward the sound. Milly was wagging her suitcase outside the window, clearly not convinced her life was in jeopardy. "You might need this someday."

Beau altered directions and plucked the suitcase from the girl with a nod of thanks.

"Hey, stud-muffin," Milly called after Beau, "you have any brothers?"

Beau chuckled, but if he responded, Amy couldn't hear, because the bus chose that minute to belch out a roaring backfire. A second later, it began to chug away—abandoning her alone in the wilderness with a crazy man.

She watched the vehicle grow smaller and smaller in the distance as she bounced along on her captor's shoulder. "Who—who do you think you are—Bronco Billy?"

"Shut up, Amy."

"*What!*"

"Which part of *shut up* don't you understand?"

"Don't tell me to shut up, you *snake*. The next bus doesn't come by for three days. What do you expect me to do?"

"I expect you to miss it."

She twisted around, rewarded only with a view of the back of his Stetson. "Put me down, you bully!"

She grabbed his hat and swatted his thigh with it. "You'd better get your testosterone checked. I think you're *way* over your quota!" She abruptly found herself settled in his saddle. She blinked in surprise, but regained her senses quickly. "That's better. Now, before you go, point this thing at the nearest police station."

Retrieving his hat from her fingers, he planted it low on his brow. "Sit forward while I get mounted."

"I will not!"

He strapped her suitcase to the saddle, casting her a skeptical look. "I may be a little heavy for you, but if you insist." Placing a boot in the stirrup, he swung himself up. Panicked, she launched herself at the horse's neck. The stallion whinnied and shook his mane at the unexpected weight, but before she toppled head over heels into the snow, she found herself in Beau's lap.

"What's wrong with you?" she cried, wishing she didn't relish the feel of his body against hers. "Has the cold driven you berserk? You do realize it's against the law to hold a person hostage!"

"I thought you wanted to be a rancher's wife," he whispered near her ear.

"I changed my mind," she lied, nervous flutterings prickling her chest.

"Why? Don't you like ranch life?"

Wary of his tricks, she wrenched around to glower at him. "I—I *hate* ranch life."

A sardonic brow rose. "And I suppose you hate Wyoming, too?"

"I *do*. I hate Wyoming with all my heart." No longer able to look him in the eye, she spun away.

"Is there anything else you hate with all your heart?" he queried softly. "Or anyone?"

Her face burned with indignation. "What is this, one last humiliation for the road?"

"Don't change the subject." He aimed his stallion toward a stand of denuded cottonwoods and snow-heavy pines. "I asked if there was anything or anyone out here you hated with all your heart. Besides mountain oysters."

Rancor rose in her like a geyser. How dare he play with her this way. Feeling thwarted and lost, she snapped, "I hate *you* with all my heart!"

"That's too bad," he said, his tone lower, huskier. "Because there's something I have to tell you. Something that has to do with the way I feel about you."

She shifted to eye him suspiciously. "You've made your feelings pretty clear. You hate me."

His half grin was rueful. "No. Not you, Amy. Never you." His tone was gentle, almost apologetic, and her frown deepened with confusion. "I hated what I thought you were. I wanted to hate you, so I made your life miserable. But you tried so hard, I couldn't find anything about you to hate. I almost told you that night in the snow, but when you said you were in love, it made me—well . . ." His jaw worked. "I vowed to have nothing to do with you after that. But when Snapper rode out to tell me you were leaving on the bus—"

"Snapper told you?"

She was swaying awkwardly as the horse high-stepped through the snow. He hugged her securely against him. "Apparently Cookie told Archie, and he told everybody else. I'd ridden out to check fence. It seems everyone on the damned ranch was looking for me to give me the news." He shifted the reins, altering their direction. "I guess they all hoped you and I would get together."

She couldn't stand it any longer, and swung one leg over the saddle horn so she could more easily read his face. Riding sideways, she peered directly at him, asking hesitantly, "They wanted *us* . . . ?" The revelation was so startling, she couldn't finish.

He nodded, his expression somber. "When I found out you were going away—not marrying Ira—I had to see you. Because if you love my father, I need to know why you're leaving without marrying him."

She saw something new in his eyes, a bright shimmer of vulnerability. The sight was so breathtaking everything inside her went still, and she knew at last her heart needed to be heard. "I don't love your father."

He hesitated, his eyes narrowing. "But I saw love in your eyes."

She shook her head, her lips lifting with melancholy. "You asked me if I was in love. And I was— I *am*. Only—not with your father."

He leaned forward, his lips very near hers. "Then who do you love, Amy?" he whispered.

She closed her eyes, unable to put her feelings into words. "I'm not sure kidnapping me off a bus gives you the right to ask."

"I do have that right," he said, his voice colored by urgency. Perplexed, her gaze shot to his. "Because I love you more than life itself, and I have to find out if you could ever give a damn about me." He brushed her lips with a gentle kiss. "I think I fell in love with you the moment I saw you in that store." He angled his face to the sky, exhaling tiredly. "I wanted you right there, but when I found out you were my father's fiancée, I went a little crazy." He shook his head. "I'm sorry I took out my frustrations on you."

She stared, hardly aware that they'd entered a secluded wood. High above them, bare cottonwood branches stirred and pine boughs bobbed, raining snow on their heads like cold little kisses.

He considered her quietly as they rode, concern etched on his handsome face. After a time, his lips lifted in a wary smile. "I see now why the silent treatment can be torture."

She lowered her gaze, unable to believe the magnitude of what he'd just told her. Trying to convince herself she wasn't dreaming, she drank in his marvelous, male scent, snuggled within his protective embrace. He was really here, really holding her, really whispering the words she'd lost all hope of hearing.

Lifting a shy glance, she was startled to see that his face was indistinct before her, and she blinked back tears of gladness. "I—I love you...." she whispered, fearing she would explode if she didn't finally say it aloud. "I always have, Beau—and I always will."

He dipped his head for a second, as though in thankful prayer, then gathered her more securely against him.

The way they fitted together was intoxicating, and hot desire sang in her veins. When he lowered his face to hers, she joyfully kissed the man for whom she had so long harbored a love more boundless than the Wyoming sky. From the first time she saw him—as angry, powerful and awe inspiring as the blizzard that brought them together—she had sensed it, but had been afraid to face the truth.

His lips were gentle, coaxing, more thrilling than anything they had shared before. Hugging him to her, she couldn't control her outcry of delight. "Oh, Beau..." she sighed against his lips, feeling a sense of completeness, a rightness. This was where she belonged. She knew she would always find a haven in Beau's arms, and he would find one in hers.

"I want you to marry me as soon as possible," he said, his voice a delicious rumble. "But if you'd rather, we can wait until Mary comes to live with us."

Amy lifted her face away to look at this most remarkable man. Her heart was so full of happiness, she couldn't help but tease, "Ah, but aren't you sending me to France?"

"Not a chance, sweetheart." His grin was so sexy it made her skin prickle with delight. "Someday, we'll go—with Mary *and* our children."

She accepted his kisses with the eager abandon of a woman who has finally found her true love and was no longer afraid to show the depth of her feelings.

Beau chuckled. "By the way, Desiree's been a pain since you left."

She traced his lips with her tongue, teasing, "I hear you were, too."

He laughed, then surprised her by slipping from the saddle and lifting her after him. "Have you ever made love in the snow?"

Her body grew hot with expectation as he shrugged off his coat and spread it in a sunny spot among the trees. "Won't we freeze?" she asked, her voice breathy with yearning.

"I won't let you get cold." He grinned that dimpled grin that made her melt, and drew her onto the coat. "But we might cause an early thaw."

A soft giggle rose in her throat, and she lifted her arms around his neck, gazing into soft blue eyes so full of deep, sweet emotion the sight took her to a place of contentment she'd never known existed.

He gathered her in his arms, murmuring erotic promises. She closed her eyes, moaning luxuriously as his knowing hands began to pleasure and arouse, his touch almost unbearable in its tenderness.

On this Wyoming winter afternoon, Beau Diablo taught Amy very intimately what passionate commitment was. And Amy knew deep in her soul she would rejoice in the learning—today and forevermore....

UNLOCK THE DOOR TO GREAT ROMANCE
AT BRIDE'S BAY RESORT

Join Harlequin's new across-the-lines series, set
in an exclusive hotel on an island off the coast of
South Carolina.

Seven of your favorite authors will bring you exciting stories
about fascinating heroes and heroines discovering love at
Bride's Bay Resort.

Look for these fabulous stories coming to a store near you
beginning in January 1996.

Visit Bride's Bay Resort each month wherever
Harlequin books are sold.

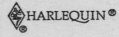

BBAYG

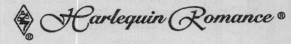

Harlequin Romance ®

New from Harlequin Romance
a very special six-book series by

MIDNIGHT SONS

DEBBIE MACOMBER

The town of Hard Luck, Alaska, needs women!

The O'Halloran brothers, who run a bush-plane service
called Midnight Sons, are heading a campaign to
attract women to Hard Luck. *(Location: north of the
Arctic Circle. Population: 150—mostly men!)*

"Debbie Macomber's *Midnight Sons* series is a delightful
romantic saga. And each book is a powerful, engaging story
in its own right. Unforgettable!"

—Linda Lael Miller

TITLE IN THE MIDNIGHT SONS SERIES:

DMS-1

Yo amo novelas con corazón!

Starting this March, Harlequin opens up to a whole new world of readers with two new romance lines in SPANISH!

Harlequin Deseo
- passionate, sensual and exciting stories

Harlequin Bianca
- romances that are fun, fresh and very contemporary

With four titles a month, each line will offer the same wonderfully romantic stories that you've come to love—now available in Spanish.

Look for them at selected retail outlets.

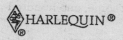

HARLEQUIN®

SPANT

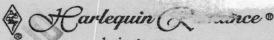
Harlequin Romance ®

brings you

How the West was Wooed!

We've rounded up twelve of our most popular authors,
and the result is a whole year of romance, Western
style. Every month we'll be bringing you a spirited,
independent woman whose heart is about to be lassoed
by a rugged, handsome, one-hundred-percent cowboy!
Watch for...

• March: **CLANTON'S WOMAN**—Patricia Knoll

• April: **A DANGEROUS MAGIC**—Patricia Wilson

• May: **THE BADLANDS BRIDE**—Rebecca Winters

• June: **RUNAWAY WEDDING**—Ruth Jean Dale

• July: **A RANCH, A RING AND EVERYTHING**—Val Daniels